She opened her eyes and there was Blane

"So this is where you've been while I was searching for you!" he remarked. He took off his jacket and wrapped it around her. "I'm going to leave you for a while to bring the car nearer," he explained.

"Go ahead," she said quickly. "I'm all right, now that you've found me."

When he returned, he carried her to the car and laid her on the back seat. "I seem to have given you a lot of trouble," she said.

His face broke into a smile. "You're much too valuable an asset to the Lennox Riding School to be left to perish in a quarry."

"Thanks," she said huffily. "I'm glad to know I'm of some value to you."

"Were you expecting a courtly compliment?" He laughed. "Surely, Briony, you know me better than that."

HENRIETTA REID
is also the author of these
Harlequin Romances

Many of these books are available at your local bookseller.

For a free catalog listing all titles currently available,
send your name and address to:

HARLEQUIN READER SERVICE
1440 South Priest Drive, Tempe, AZ 85281.
Canadian address: Stratford, Ontario N5A 6W2

New Boss at Birchfields

by

HENRIETTA REID

Harlequin Books

TORONTO • NEW YORK • LOS ANGELES • LONDON
AMSTERDAM • PARIS • SYDNEY • HAMBURG
STOCKHOLM • ATHENS • TOKYO • MILAN

Original hardcover edition published in 1982
by Mills & Boon Limited

ISBN 0-373-02524-6

Harlequin Romance first edition January 1983

CHAPTER ONE

BRIONY pulled her coat collar closer against her cheeks. It was cold waiting for Jeremy. Perhaps it would be better to go a little way down the street and not shelter within the office doorway. It would look to the staff as they streamed out as if she was waiting anxiously and expectantly for his appearance.

For undoubtedly Jeremy was popular. Too popular perhaps for his own good, she realised, with a little wry twist to her mouth. And yet—oh well, she might as well admit it to herself, she was madly, crazily in love with him. Whenever any of those niggling little doubts intruded she forced them firmly into the background of her mind.

She took a few steps along the street, stamping her feet to keep the circulation going. Then as she swung around to face the façade of Stanton, Hodges & Company, the accountancy firm that they both worked for, she saw him come out on to the stone steps accompanied by a couple of girls from the typing pool. They were hanging on to his arms and gazing up into his face, evidently enraptured by the attention he was impartially giving them. He was smiling with that special teasing look which Briony knew was one of his main attractions.

She touched the tiny circle of sapphires on the slender gold band of her engagement ring, as though to reassure herself. After all, why should it worry her that he was always the centre of interest as far as the other girls in the office were concerned, when Jeremy and herself were already making plans for their marriage! She shrugged off the nagging doubts which so often nowadays assailed

5

her. Probably pre-wedding nerves, she told herself. She watched as Jeremy waved to the girls before they set off giggling at some parting quip he had made.

He approached her with his rapid impatient stride. It was quite easy to see by the very way he carried himself that Jeremy was a man who was going places, and that he saw nothing but success when he looked to the future.

As soon as he joined her he tucked her arm into his and together they walked off in the direction of the tube station. But his silence was in marked contrast to the good-humour he had shown her colleagues before he parted from them. She gazed up at him, troubled and uncertain, then tried a few remarks, only to be answered by abstracted monosyllables.

Briony felt her heart sink. This was not the first time she had seen Jeremy in this strange uncommunicative mood. And lately she had become timid of pestering him for an explanation. She dreaded his offputting frown and sharp rejoinder. It was his way of letting her know that she was treading on dangerous ground. And it puzzled and distressed her when she realised that he regarded her questions as an intrusion.

He hesitated as they came to the short flight of steps leading down to the tube station, and she felt a little sickening sense of disappointment as she saw that he had no intention of going farther with her.

'But aren't you coming back to tea, Jeremy? Mum is making something particularly special. You know how she loves experimenting with recipes! And they do usually turn out wonderfully, don't they?' she added desperately. Jeremy was a great favourite with Mrs Walton, who usually excelled herself when she thought he would be dropping in for tea on his way back from the office with Briony.

'No, I'm afraid I'll have to skip it tonight,' he replied a little impatiently. He patted his bulging briefcase. 'I'll have to tackle this little lot as soon as I get home. It seems to me I'm getting more and more responsibility these days!'

But she could see from his self-satisfied expression that he wasn't at all displeased at the extra work.

'You mean you'd rather be at home with your papers than be with me?' she demanded desperately.

'But don't you see, Briony, this means there's a future for me in the Company! Promotion would mean the whole difference to our plans, so for heaven's sake stop standing there like a picture of woe and hurry home!'

'But surely it won't take you *all* night?' she persisted. 'And we've so many arrangements to discuss about the wedding!'

'Even if it doesn't take me all night, what about it? We can't be jawing all the time about the colour of the bridesmaids' dresses and stuff like that! There are other things to see to.'

'But what other things have you to see to? I mean, apart from the extra work from the office. It seems to me you've been different recently—as if—well, as if you were losing interest in planning our future life together.'

'Oh, don't be such an ass, Briony!' he retorted irritably. 'Surely a man has a right to some life of his own, even if——'

'Even if he's going to tie himself to someone else for life! Isn't that what you mean?' she ended fiercely. 'It's not as if I expect you to be with me every moment of the day. Anyway, how could it be? You and I are in completely different worlds in the office.'

'And that's a world I don't intend to remain in much longer,' he put in.

'What on earth do you mean?' she asked, bewildered.

He clapped his briefcase. 'This may be nothing but boring work to you, but to me it's the future. It means we'll be going places, you and I, right to the top.'

'Oh, I know you're ambitious,' she said contritely.

'But isn't it a pity to throw away the present for something that may never happen at all?'

'What do you mean?' he asked sharply. 'But of course it will happen! If I want it to, it will. And if I work hard enough and am allowed to keep my mind clear of all those stupid, niggling little details that you seem to find so important, like what size the wedding cake is to be and what relations are to be invited, and all the hundred and one things that are just holding me back. Anyway, it's your business to take care of all those details, isn't it? Why drag me into it?'

'I suppose I have been a bit selfish,' Briony sighed. 'It's just—well, I suppose I wanted to share things with you.'

'Well, don't,' he told her, 'for I haven't the slightest interest in it. I just wish we could run off together somewhere and get married without all this fuss and bother, and get back to work immediately after the honeymoon.'

Briony was silent for a moment. She felt a coldness come over her. Was Jeremy not rather overdoing his man of business act? Surely, if he loved her, he would be looking forward to his wedding day as much as she was!

'You're regretting it, isn't that it, Jeremy?' she said flatly. 'There's someone else. Why don't you admit it?'

Suddenly she found herself wildly possessive and a raging jealousy seemed to tear at her heart-strings. It would be one of the girls in the office, she thought. But which one? Was it possible she was an object of pity or ridicule to the other girls? The thought burned like acid.

'Now you're being ridiculous!' he replied contemptuously. 'You're being a typical female—always assuming that a girl must be involved in a man's life somehow or other! What's wrong with you, Briony, is that you're much too romantic. You seem to think life ought to be a perpetual love affair!'

'No, I don't!' she told him furiously. 'But I notice how different you are now. You used to be fun to be with, and I know you're still the same to the other girls. But when it comes to me it's a different matter. It's as though—as though you were trying to put me off—as if you regret you ever got involved with me.'

She felt as if she was going to burst into bitter tears, and was appalled by the thought. To let Jeremy see she cared so much would only increase his exasperation with her.

She took out her hanky and blew her nose furiously. 'I'd better go,' she said flatly. 'Perhaps I'll see you tomorrow evening.' She tried to sound indifferent, but her eyes, watching him, brimmed with unshed tears.

He hesitated uneasily. 'Well, no, not tomorrow, Briony. In fact not for the next few days. I'm really going to be terribly busy. And take my word for that and don't let your imagination run wild.'

'I see.' The tears she had vainly tried to hold back misted her eyes.

'And don't begin crying, for heaven's sake! Look, if you insist on knowing what it's all about, here goes. But remember I wanted to break this to you gently later on. But since you're so darned set on having the truth— well, here it is, and you've only got yourself to blame if it comes as a shock. I've just been told that I've been posted to Aberdeen.'

'What!' It was as though he had dealt her a stunning blow. As though in a dream she could feel the surge of the rush-hour crowd swarm past them, dividing as they passed them and then meeting again in a stream as they hurried off to their homes in the suburbs.

'But that's miles and miles away,' she said in a whisper. 'Why, it's away in the north of Scotland.'

'That's true,' Jeremy agreed. 'But there are plenty of opportunities there. You know we're opening a new office, and why shouldn't I be one of the first to go now that the Company has such confidence in me? Aberdeen's a great international centre now, full of wealthy oil-men. The kind of place a man could go as high as he wanted.'

'But I simply don't understand,' Briony told him with growing bewilderment. 'Do you mean you were simply asked if you would go, without their knowing what your plans were?'

For a moment he looked slightly uncomfortable. 'Well, no, as a matter of fact, I put in to be posted.'

'You put in for it without even telling me?' Anger overcame her bitter disappointment. 'Do you really mean you arranged to start a new life there before you knew whether I would like to live there or not?' Her voice rose shrilly.

'But why not?' he demanded. 'I'm ambitious. I want to be where the action is. Do you really want me to be stuck in the same old office with the same old gang around until we're all ancient? Don't you want me to mix around with lots of wealthy and influential people? I might even be invited to the States if I meet the right people and play my cards well!'

'But what about me? Have you, even for one moment, considered my point of view?' Briony insisted.

'Yes, of course!' he replied impatiently. 'But I assumed this would be best—for both of us, I mean. All it will mean is that you'll have to be patient for a while—wait until I've found my feet there and become established. You don't think I'm doing this just for myself, do you? I'm trying to make a new way of life for us both, and as soon as I've found a firm footing there I'll send for you and you can join me. You must realise that having a wife to support wouldn't be a good idea—at the beginning, anyway.'

'I see!' Briony felt stunned as the full realisation of his plans swept over her. 'In other words, you were going to break it gently to me that we were not to get married until you'd established yourself. Well, at any rate, this explains your lack of interest in the wedding plans!' she concluded tonelessly.

Her bitterness silenced Jeremy, then he said awkwardly, 'I might have to travel quite a lot and there would be plenty of extra paper-work, so my evenings would be full. Besides, a man like me, if he wanted to get on, would have to be available. I mean,' he added with an attempt at a laugh, 'I could hardly say, I'm sorry, sir, I can't fly off to Saudi Arabia. My wife's holding a tea-party tomorrow.'

'No, I suppose not,' Briony agreed flatly.

'There, you see!' he remarked, as though he had solved their problems in the best possible manner. 'By far the wisest thing would be for me to go ahead and prepare a home for you.'

'But how am I going to live without you?' Briony wailed.

'We'll just have to make do with letters and phone calls—for a while at least,' he said. 'Do buck up, Briony. It won't be as bad as you think. And maybe occasionally I could snatch a visit down South.'

There was a sickening finality about his words that made her realise the hopelessness of any further argument, and without replying she turned away, desolate at heart, and ran swiftly down the steps.

Jeremy hesitated for a moment and then followed her. 'Why must you take everything so seriously?' he demanded as he caught up with her. 'Remember, time will pass very quickly, and, as I said, if I get the chance, I'll pop down often to see you.'

She didn't answer.

But before she got into the carriage he caught her by the shoulders and kissed her warmly, and she felt all the irresistible charm of his personality sweep over her. If only by some stroke of magic he would change his mind, become satisfied with his position in the office and be content to look forward later to a modest promotion!

She found a seat by the window and watched his receding figure through a blur of tears, hoping against hope that he would give a reassuring wave of the hand and that smile of his! But already, with swift impatient strides, he was being lost in the eddying crowd.

Afterwards, she was never to forget the misery of the short train journey to the small semi-detached house which she shared with her widowed mother. She found herself feverishly turning and twisting the ring on her third finger. Did it really mean anything now? she wondered. And yet how happy she had been the day they had bought it together!

'It's really not very much, darling,' he had whispered when the shop assistant had placed it in its velvet case. 'But later on, wait and see, I'll cover you with diamonds and pearls.'

She had laughed delightedly. 'No, that's not for me! I'm simply not the type. I'm small and a bit on the skinny side. This suits me perfectly and I'll never want anything else in its place.'

'That's what you say now,' he told her. 'But what woman wouldn't be delighted to have that knuckle-duster over there?' He had pointed to an enormous solitaire diamond laid on its velvet bed under a thick glass case. 'Don't tell me you wouldn't get a kick out of showing your girl friends something like that?'

'Really, Jeremy,' she had laughed, 'hasn't it dawned on you that I'm not at all the regal type? No, these little sapphires are just perfect, and the girls will be green with envy when I show the ring to them.'

It had been his turn to laugh then and he had sounded a little self-satisfied as he said deprecatingly, 'Well, I hope I haven't broken too many hearts by choosing you!'

'You know perfectly well you have,' she had told him severely. 'And by the way, you'll have to give up playing the field when we're married. I know it's only fun to you, and you don't mean any of them to take you seriously, but I'll be madly jealous and probably create the most awful scenes.'

He had given her shoulders a little squeeze. 'You're not the scene-making type. That's what I like about you! Anyway, once we're married you can chuck up your job.'

'I think I'd like that,' she had replied with a happy little sigh. 'It's definitely not my idea of heaven anyway.'

'Then that's settled! And now what about celebrating?'

In spite of her protests he had tucked her arm under his and had marched her to the best restaurant in the town. 'You may as well get used to this kind of living,' he had told her, 'because one of these days this is the only sort of place you and I are going to be seen at.'

She had really taken him seriously. To her it had been an unusual and exciting adventure, in keeping with the feeling of a new beginning and the comforting feeling of that gold band and the cluster of tiny sapphires on the third finger of her left hand.

It was after Jeremy's departure that the feeling of his ring on her finger gave her less and less comfort. To begin with, his letters were few and far between and when she did devour them eagerly she was always left with a sense of let-down, for they gave an impression of frantic activity. Even the endearments were written in a hasty scrawl, as though inserted at the last moment to humour her. His letters, she soon found, were full of the stories of his triumphs and the complimentary remarks he had overheard or had been conveyed to him by other members of the staff.

It was her mother who seemed to take pleasure in these passages when she passed them across the breakfast table. 'Jeremy seems to be doing very well,' she would say with satisfaction. 'I always knew that young man was going places. You're a lucky girl, Briony. He'll make you a fine husband.'

But as Briony took his letters back, she felt only desolation. She felt that he was growing further and further away from her, his interests widening, and that soon she would be nothing more to him than the memory of a pretty girl whom he had known for a while. To her mother, of course, it seemed that Jeremy was busily preparing a nest for her only child, but it was clear to Briony herself that as far as Jeremy was concerned it was a case of out of sight, out of mind.

She found too that when the girls in the office questioned her she had to try to sound airy and confident. She even found herself indulging in gentle fantasies. Oh yes, she would tell them, Jeremy was coming back the following weekend and they were going on a short walking tour. She even began to devise more romantic outings—a cruise around the Hebrides, perhaps, as soon as he had time. But gradually she became more and more frantic. The months were passing and still he had made no reference to marriage, or discussed their plans in any way. What did he really feel about her? Had he met someone else, perhaps? She simply had to know.

At work she was preoccupied and absentminded, and the girls joked about her being lovesick. But Briony knew that if she didn't pull herself together and find out exactly where she stood with Jeremy she would indeed find herself out of work. She would go to Aberdeen, meet him and find out how he felt about her. This would force him to take some definite stand—especially if she were to tell him she had thrown up her job to be with him. It would be a desperate gamble, but anything would be better than her present dreadful uncertainty.

When at last she told her mother of her plan Mrs Walton was anything but enthusiastic. 'It seems to me you're not really giving Jeremy much time to establish himself, are you? You know, you may regret acting so hastily, Briony. Men hate being run after, and Jeremy is no exception.'

'But I'm not running after him! Don't you see that?' Briony put in quickly. 'I can easily get a job in the North. Jeremy told me it's full of opportunities.'

'Yes, but your real reason is to find out where you stand with him, isn't it? What you want to do is keep an eye on him, as it were. You can't deny that.'

To a certain extent this was true, Briony knew, yet, knowing Jeremy as she did, she felt justified in trying to find out where she stood with him. All the same, her mother's words had struck close to the truth, and when she told them at the office about her plans she was disconcerted to find how very well informed they were about her private affairs.

'Are you not being a very foolish young lady to act so precipitously?' the elderly man behind the big desk asked her. 'The office grapevine tells me you're leaving us to go to Aberdeen.'

But Briony was adamant. By this time she was truly desperate. And she had a steely determination to use the fact that she had thrown up her job as a weapon in eliciting from Jeremy his real intentions.

To her relief her mother, though still disapproving, had begun to accept the situation with resignation. All that remained now was to pack her bags, phone Jeremy and let him know when she would be arriving. She booked a place in a second-class sleeping compartment and before the train left she put in a phone call to Jeremy.

But the call was not at all reassuring.

'What are you thinking of?' he asked sharply, when she told him of her plan.

'Simply that your letters recently haven't been very satisfactory, and I think we should meet and thrash things out.'

'What on earth has come over you, Briony? What is there to thrash out?'

'What I mean is that I'm taking the night train,' she told him desperately, trying to keep her voice firm and even. 'If you care for me at all you'll try to meet it.'

'Don't do it, Briony!' His voice was sharp. 'Wait for my letter—I'll explain everything.'

'If I don't rush I'll miss my train,' she replied, before slamming down the phone.

Later on, as the train sped through the night and she dozed and awoke, she felt a sense of adventure alternating with hope and despair. What would have been in his letter? she wondered. Would it have confirmed her fondest hopes, or would the message have been that everything was over between them?

The scenery changed from the warmth of the South to the desolate mountains of the North, made more frightening by the moonlight, and she knew she was moving into a strange and unknown world. The thought was both attractive and terrifying. Perhaps Jeremy had already made good and they would be able to get married right away. Even if this were not possible, perhaps she could stay in Aberdeen, be near him, see him every day. Jeremy with his talent for getting along with all sorts of people was bound to have plenty of contacts. He would be able to find her a suitable job so that they need never be parted again.

Long before the train reached Aberdeen she was awake and dressed. She took particular care with her make-up and felt confident that her new tweed suit was eminently suitable for a Highland holiday.

As the train slowed and drew into the station she stared out eagerly. There was no sign of Jeremy, but she felt certain he was somewhere in the crowd. Carrying her suitcase, she stood on the platform beside the carriage door. Sooner or later he would find her. But as time passed and chatting groups dispersed coldness struck at her heart. She felt isolated, as though deserted on a desert island. Her case in her hand, she stood searching the departing crowd, but there was no one even remotely resembling Jeremy. Perhaps, she thought, grasping at straws, he was delayed.

She took a seat on the platform, determined to sit it out. But as time passed, she realised with sick dismay that Jeremy was definitely not going to greet her. There was no sign of his blond hair and laughing eyes. There was only one thing for it—she would have to go to his office. He would probably have a simple explanation for his absence and all her silly worries would evaporate.

She checked in her suitcase and took a taxi to his business address. She was immediately overawed by the size of the building. For a moment she stood in the palatial entrance with its gleaming polished granite walls and mosaic floor wondering where in this vast office building she could locate Jeremy. But now her spirits were rising. It was plain that Jeremy was doing well. He must have many important appointments and commitments.

She turned into the building and was crossing the wide floor when a lift door opened and Jeremy, preceded by an extremely elegant-looking young woman carrying a file, got out. The girl was speaking over her shoulder intimately to him, and Jeremy, Briony could see with a little twinge at her heart, was as usual turning on the charm. How ordinary her new tweed suit seemed in comparison to the restrained elegance of this tall young woman, her dark hair swept back and gathered into a glossy chignon!

With a few parting words and a brilliant smile the girl went off along a corridor, and Jeremy caught sight of Briony.

His face stiffened as he hurried towards her. He took her by the arm and led her outside. 'What on earth are you doing here?' he grated. 'I thought I told you on the phone not to come.'

'But I told you I was leaving on the overnight train,' she replied.

'Well, I simply couldn't believe it,' he told her. 'What could you have been thinking of, to do such a mad thing?' He looked at her keenly. 'You haven't by any chance flung up your job, have you?'

Briony could feel her cheeks grow pale at the tone of contempt in his voice, but she pulled herself together. This was no time to show weakness. 'Yes, I have,' she retorted. 'And what about it?'

'What about it!' he repeated incredulously. 'Just what do you think is going to become of you now?'

'But there must be loads of jobs in Aberdeen,' she faltered. 'You said in your letters that there are un-limited opportunities and——'

'There are loads of opportunities for *qualified* people, especially for people with very unusual qualifications,' he grated. 'But as far as ordinary run-of-the-mill people, well—— I'm afraid, Briony, you'll have to face the fact that there's no future for you here.'

'So you don't care any more,' she said through stiff lips.

He hesitated. 'Well, if you want it straight from the shoulder, no, I don't care any more!'

CHAPTER TWO

'So you've met someone else,' she said tonelessly after a long moment of silence. She nodded towards the door through which the girl with the shining dark hair had disappeared. 'She's beautiful—and wealthy too! Isn't that it?' At last the veils had been taken from her eyes. She saw Jeremy as he really was and she no longer hoped.

'Do you know who that girl is?' he asked in a low tone. 'She's the sister of Slim Morgan, a Texan with more money than you'd dream about in a thousand years! He'd promised me a place in his organisation. It's world-wide and growing every moment.'

'And there's no place for me in your life any more,' Briony said disconsolately. 'I can see, Jeremy, that I didn't understand you. I thought you were warmhearted and that everything was for laughs. You understand yourself better—you said you were going ahead. Well, this is the end, isn't it?' She pulled the ring from her finger and handed it to him.

'And what am I to do with this?' Jeremy asked, looking down at the cheap little ring lying in the palm of his hand.

'You can give it to Miss Morgan,' Briony said in a low voice. 'And I only hope she'll appreciate it as much as I did.'

She swung around and marched towards the door, her head held high.

Once on the pavement she felt her eyes cloud with tears. She hurried along, mixing with the crowd in Union Street, gazing into the shop windows through a blur of tears.

Gradually she got a grip on herself. She would cry later. After all, this was something that had been a dark cloud on her mind for a long time.

She paused in front of a big dress shop trying to look interested in the window display. What was she to do now? To think that she had relied on Jeremy to help her to find a job! Why she wasn't even fixed up with accommodation for the night. There was, of course, her godmother, Hettie Gillies. She had promised her mother she would visit her. But Briony had visualised herself accompanied by Jeremy. It would have made a pleasant day's outing, for Hettie lived in a beautiful wooded village along the valley of the Dee. Now she would be visiting her in very different circumstances. How would Hettie receive her? She remembered holidays at Birchfields when she was a child and recollected that Hettie could be a little sharp-tongued at times. But there was nothing for it but to fling herself on her godmother's mercy and hope for the best.

Recklessly she decided to travel by taxi. The driver gave her a faint look of surprise because Abergour was some distance from the town, but she felt she simply could not economise that day. Better to know how things stood as soon as possible. If Hettie was unable to put her up then she would be forced to take the next train home. In a few days it would be common knowledge among their friends and acquaintances that she had thrown up her job for a man who had rejected her. She shrank back in the seat of the taxi at the very thought.

As the taxi moved out through the suburbs she hardly saw the granite houses with their pretty well-tended gardens, and as they left Aberdeen behind the beauty of the countryside meant nothing to her. She stared blankly at the loveliness of birches and rowans, the rushing streams and wooded slopes.

It was only as they drew near to the village of

Abergour that she pulled herself together and looked about for her first glimpse of Birchfields. For a moment her view was obscured by a giant hoarding on which was written 'Lennox Riding School' in enormous lettering. Then, once again, she craned her neck seeking the untidy grounds that surrounded Birchfields.

Roy and Hettie Gillies had bought Birchfields, which had once been the home of a wealthy Aberdeen merchant. They had not had money enough to keep the large Victorian house in good condition, and Briony remembered it as rather shabby, the carpets worn and the curtains slightly dusty. But Hettie had the gift of making the house a warm and welcoming place, and Briony looked back with happiness to the holidays she had spent there as a child. Into her mind flashed the memory of the scent of baking in the large old-fashioned untidy kitchen. Roy and Hettie, childless themselves, had opened their hearts to the eager little girl with the bright red hair who had romped in the garden with the dogs and helped to pick the sun-ripened strawberries and had helped to pack the bunches of flowers that the Gillies had sold in Aberdeen.

Roy had managed a market garden with the help of a boy, Hettie helping out when they were particularly busy. But now Roy was dead and Hettie would be alone in the big house. Briony felt a little stab of recognition as she caught a glimpse of the village church with its great clock still stopped at ten past six. 'The gate of Birchfields is somewhere along here to the left,' she told the driver. But she felt confused. Instead of the familiar wall with its lichen-covered stones they were passing white railings through which she could see a paddock in which ponies were grazing.

'Perhaps we'd better stop here,' she said doubtfully to the driver.

She gazed about in bewilderment. Where were the great iron gates with the word Birchfields worked in wrought-iron? It had disappeared. Now all that appeared was a low gate that matched the white rails which now enclosed the grounds. Although 'enclosed' was hardly the word, because the rails were so widely spaced as to afford a full vista of grounds completely flat on which were stabling, paddocks, and in the background a house which seemed not at all to resemble the sprawling outlines of the house she had known as a child. It had a neat, freshly-scrubbed look with shining windows and formal flowerbeds, and in the background could be seen a gigantic Dutch barn only half erected, on which workmen were still busy.

To one side of the gate was another of those huge signs with 'Lennox Riding School' written on it. This time there was also a hand pointing along the broad gravelled driveway.

Briony gazed at the scene uneasily. There was something almost nightmarish about this strange metamorphosis, as though the house she had remembered had been nothing more than a dream.

'You'd better wait,' she told the driver. 'I'm not sure this is the right place.'

Slowly she opened the gate and walked along the drive. On either side the grass was trimly mown and everything seemed smooth and orderly. Much too orderly to belong to Hettie, she thought with growing dismay.

Off to one side was a row of stables, and these too had a severity of outline and complete lack of disorder that somehow added to her unease.

As she drew level a boy emerged from one of the half-doors. He closed and bolted the top portion and turned towards her enquiringly.

'I'm looking for Mrs Gillies,' she told him. 'She used to live at Birchfields, but somehow I can't——'

She paused and he said, 'This is Birchfields, or used to be, but it's Mr Lennox's place now.'

'So I see,' she replied a little acidly. 'I saw the notice at the gates.'

'Yes, he bought it from her, and now the old lady lives at Amulree Cottage. It's the second from the end after you pass the shop.'

Briony heard the news with a sense of relief. So at least Hettie still lived in Abergour. She had had a curious superstitious dread that in some mysterious way Hettie had disappeared off the face of the earth.

'Oh, I'll find it all right,' she said quickly. 'I used to live here when I was a child. I don't suppose the village has changed much.'

But she was to find that this was not entirely true as, once again in the taxi, she was driven through the village. It seemed to her now that it was rather a busier place. Outside several of the cottages there were signs— 'Teas', 'Bed and breakfast'. And in place of the old tiny village shop there was now a larger double-windowed erection, hanging in the doorway of which she spotted a big bunch of fisherman's waders.

Set back from the street was the old parish church of weathered stone, the stained glass of the windows looking dull from the outside. But she remembered how wonderfully brilliant it could look on a Sunday morning when the sun was streaming through and sending down shafts of blues and greens, reds and golds on the mosaic of the aisles. Eventually as the village petered out they came to the few remaining detached cottages. At first glance it would have been hard to tell which of these belonged to Hettie Gillies. Each had an untidy garden with untrimmed shrubs and wandering roses and tangled country flowers. But on one of these was the name Amulree Cottage on a slatted wooden plaque.

'Here we are!' Briony paid off the taxi, took her case and walked quickly along the short brick pathway.

The door stood slightly ajar as she knocked and from the interior came the delicious scent of oven-fresh pastry. She knocked again, but the only response was the sound of an oven door being banged somewhere at the back of the cottage, and a faint humming of someone going about their work in a preoccupied manner.

Briony poked her head inside and immediately found herself in the living-room of the little house.

A small wood fire crackled in the black-leaded grate. A comfortable chintz-covered armchair was drawn up on either side of this. Then her eyes lit upon the familiar china cabinet. She put down her case and crossed over to it.

Yes, there were the little Dresden vases covered with tiny blue forget-me-nots: the pair of clouded yellow bonbonneries with golden butterflies. There were other items well beloved from the days of her childhood—the serried rows of antique paperweights and the Chelsea ornaments—a boy playing a flute, and wearing a black hat with pink ribbons and a pink tunic with yellow flowers. Hettie, in days gone by, had permitted Briony to take them out and even to wash them if she was especially careful. They had delighted her when she was a child and now it was somehow comforting to see them again. It helped to alleviate the horrible feeling of rejection she had experienced after she had parted from Jeremy.

She straightened up and looked about the small cosy room. It was untidy, of course—Hettie's rooms always were! A sewing-basket spilled to one side and a pile of magazines tossed untidily on a sofa table! This was Hettie's cottage all right, and for the time being she was safe and at home.

A moment later there was the sound of footsteps and Hettie came into the room. She gazed for a moment in blank amazement at the girl who stood in the middle of the floor smiling at her, then she ran forward, flung her arms about her godchild and kissed her warmly. 'My, how you've grown! I wouldn't have known you if it hadn't been for that wonderful red hair of yours. I always said you'd grow up pretty, and now I see I was right!'

Briony had been regarding her godmother, seeing her with new eyes now that she herself was an adult. It was strange to discover that Hettie was not as tall as she had imagined her, but was in fact rather petite. Nor was she as old as she had appeared to the child, although her dark hair was sprinkled with white. She had bright high colouring and a resolute expression about her mouth and immediately gave the impression of being a little lady whom it would not be wise to trifle with.

'Come and sit by the fire.' Hettie poked it hospitably. 'You're just in time for a nice cup of tea. I've some scones new out of the oven, so we may as well have them now. And then you must tell me what's brought you to Deeside, for I've the feeling,' she added a little slyly, 'that you didn't come all this way just to visit your old godmother.'

She brushed the magazines from the table, laid a cloth and set out cups and saucers.

While they had tea Hettie questioned Briony about family affairs and Briony brought her up to date as well as she could without revealing the reason that had brought her to Aberdeen, simply saying that she would have liked to get a job here but had decided to pay a flying visit before making any decision.

But soon she discovered that she was losing Hettie's attention. There was only one subject that really interested her godmother, and that was Blane Lennox and the alterations he was making at her beloved Birchfields.

Hettie's face tightened as she asked, 'I suppose you called at Birchfields and they directed you on here?'

'Yes, I came across a boy there who told me you were living at the cottage now.' Briony forbore to add how shocked she had been to see the alterations in Birchfields.

But Hettie wasn't listening. She poked the fire, her lips pursed. 'Not that one can call it Birchfields any longer, because it doesn't exist now! There's simply nothing that he hasn't changed. I can hardly bear to pass the place now. Those horrible white railings, instead of the old walls! He bulldozed the old birchwoods and crushed the greenhouses.'

'I suppose he would need the space if he's running a riding school,' Briony said consolingly. 'The woods would probably be a hazard, especially for young pupils.'

But this was an unfortunate remark, she quickly discovered. Hettie stiffened. 'Am I to take it, then, that you prefer Birchfields as it is now?'

'No, of course not!' Briony assured her hastily. 'But if this new owner is running the place as a business he's bound to take a practical view of things.'

'Oh, he's running it as a business all right,' Hettie said dryly. 'He's turned Birchfields into a sort of horses' playground. Everything must be done for their convenience and human beings count for nothing. But then the man has no real breeding. You must have seen those great vulgar signs of his pointing out the way to his school. And this is only the beginning! I've heard from Annie Skinner—I suppose you'll hardly remember her, but she used to run the shop when you were here last.'

Briony smiled. 'I remember her all right. I used to buy soor plooms in the shop. What became of it anyway? I see there's a new shop now.'

'Not a new shop,' Hettie corrected. 'Annie still runs it. She has expanded, you see. And Annie knows everything that goes on in the village. It seems it's been arranged that some of the girls from Laureston School are to take riding lessons. Well, all I can say is I pity the poor parents. He's sure to charge sky-high fees, because he knows that only wealthy parents can afford to send their children to Laureston.'

Briony glanced across at her godmother. How bitter Hettie had become! And she wondered for a moment if it was because Hettie saw living in the cottage as a come-down in the world. 'After Roy died Birchwoods must have been too large for you to manage on your own,' she urged. 'And you seem so comfortable here, with all your own treasures about you!' She glanced at the dainty Chippendale cabinet in its place in the corner of the room.

'That's all very well and good,' Hettie replied impatiently, 'but here am I in this poky cottage while Lennox lords it up there at Birchfields! He managed to put me out of that all right! He worked for it and succeeded!'

Briony looked at her in amazement. What on earth could she mean by that last remark? But perhaps Hettie meant nothing very special. Perhaps it was no more than the outpourings of a woman who was bitter and resentful.

As though guessing her godchild's reaction, Hettie said quickly, 'But there, I'm becoming quite a bore about that man! I think, for a change, we'll do the dishes. You wash, if you like, and I'll dry.'

Goodnaturedly Briony helped her godmother to wash the tea things. And afterwards, when she was shown to her room under the eaves she found that it contained one of Hettie's treasures, a single fourposter hung with crisp muslin. Briony helped her make up the bed with snowy starched linen and a patchwork quilt.

Afterwards, when she had unpacked and arranged her clothes in the William and Mary tallboy, she told Hettie she would like to take a stroll through the village and catch up with some of the changes that had occurred since her last visit.

As she walked along she had time to consider what plans she should make for the future.

Instinctively she rejected the idea of returning home and having to confess that Jeremy had let her down. Let her down was putting it too mildly, she thought dryly. In fact, she had been jilted. She might be able to obtain a position in Aberdeen, of course, if she searched for it, but better still, it would be wonderful if she could find employment here in Abergour. Not that there was any possibility of that. It was a typical Highland community, of crofters, the land tapering out into glens with groves of birch and alder, with here and there little rivulets of water streaming down through the ferns and bracken and running in dark peaty streams along the sides of the road. This was not the type of place in which her particular training would find an outlet, she thought wryly.

She paused outside the general store with the double windows which she had noticed as she drove through the village. Inside she spotted a revolving stand with views of the surrounding countryside. She would send a card to her mother, she decided. She had picked out a view of the fairy-tale castle, Craigievar, when she heard a voice at her elbow, 'You're Briony Walton, aren't you?'

Briony swung around to find herself being surveyed by a tall, stout woman with red, scrubbed cheeks and bright enquiring eyes.

'You don't remember me,' the woman said. 'I'm Annie Skinner. I used to come to Birchfields to help sort the fruit and vegetables for the market. And that was in between serving in the shop,' she added with a chuckle.

'But of course I remember you,' Briony told her. 'I used to buy soor plooms in the shop. I suppose you don't have them now. They'll be old-fashioned, I suppose.'

'Not at all!' Annie pointed to a glass jar containing

very large boiled sweets in the shape of round green balls. 'The people here in Abergour still ask for them. But mostly I sell them to the tourists. Some of them are Scottish from way far back and remember them from their childhood. I always keep plenty in stock.'

'Soor plooms! That means sour plums, doesn't it?' Briony asked.

'Yes. There's no doubt they're a bit acid,' Annie agreed, 'but then young stomachs make light of that.'

'The shop's much larger than it was,' Briony remarked.

Annie nodded. 'Yes. I bought up the cottage next door and had another window put in. Almost like a supermarket now, isn't it? I'd have known you anywhere,' Annie pursued, 'because your hair was always that strange colour, the colour of a rowan berry, I used often say. But besides that I heard there was a stranger at Hettie's cottage, and as soon as I saw you I put two and two together.'

So Hettie was right, Briony was thinking. There was very little escaped Annie Skinner's eagle eye.

'Oh yes, there have been great changes at Abergour since you were here last,' Annie went on. 'And I won't deny that at times it's been hard to manage. But the village is becoming more and more popular with tourists, even if some of them only stop off for a little while before travelling further west. Still, all in all, I haven't done too badly, and I must admit this new Lennox Riding School has made quite a difference. You see, we all thought at first he was going to keep Birchfields on as a market garden, but when he set about tearing everything down, trees and shrubs, and to flatten the land itself and make it as smooth as a billiard table— well, it soon became clear to us he had other ideas. The next thing we knew there were those big notices by the roadside. Poor Hettie took it badly. I think she had the idea everything was going to go on as it had done before she sold it. But times change, and it's not always for the worst!'

'Yes, she seems a bit upset about it,' Briony agreed cautiously.

'But how are you getting along yourself?' Annie asked. 'Hettie was telling me you have a big job in an important firm now. She always lets me know the news when your mother writes to her at Christmas. There was some talk too that you were thinking of getting married. I think your mother wrote about that some time back. Is it true Mr Right has come along and there's going to be wedding bells very soon?'

Would it always be like this? Briony wondered, as she laughingly dismissed Annie Skinner's remarks. Would she always have to make excuses, always have to disguise the truth that Jeremy had flung her over for a girl he considered more eligible? 'You were speaking about Mr Lennox,' she put in quickly.

Luckily Mrs Skinner allowed herself to be sidetracked. 'Oh yes, some changes are for the better! Take Mr Lennox now. His coming has brought quite a bit of business to the village. And now that the children from the school are to be taught there, it will help even more. He has bought some Shetland ponies for the younger children. But he has all sorts of ponies and horses there. By all accounts he's a splendid horseman himself and has won all sorts of prizes at shows for jumping and for his fine horses too. All the same, things aren't running all too smooth for him at the moment,' she added with a tinge of satisfaction in her voice. 'He's looking for a suitable girl to teach the very young children—not that he'll be able to get anyone from Abergour to do it!'

'But why is that?' Briony enquired.

'Because no one can get along with that man,' Annie Skinner replied emphatically. 'He's a real rough diamond, you know. His word is law up there at Birchfields. More like a dictator than anything else, that's what Blane Lennox is! Oh, I can tell you there will be no one queueing up there for the job.'

But Briony was only half listening. So there was actually a job vacant in Abergour after all! Well, she might not be an expert horsewoman, but at least she would know how to lead children around on Shetland ponies. And as for Blane Lennox being difficult to get along with, she had worked for difficult people in her time. When it came to those who demanded the impossible she felt she had plenty of experience.

She was vaguely aware of Annie Skinner continuing her tirade.

'Oh yes, I've had some experience of Blane Lennox! During the winter months when there were no tourists and he was getting the house renovated, I went up—lowered myself—to ask for a job helping in the house. Well, he took me on—on trial, as it were. And though I worked myself to the bone, I couldn't give satisfaction. On the second day I was there I was put to fixing the attics. Well, I set to. Naturally I stopped off now and then for a sly cup of tea—to give myself a buck, as it were. And I must say the housekeeper was very good and made no objection. Well, what do you think, just as I was sitting at the kitchen table with a cup in my hand in he walks and as good as accuses me of loafing. Said he wouldn't have any slackers around his place. Never a word of praise, mind you! Naturally I wouldn't stand for that—and neither would the girls of Abergour. Oh yes, indeed, Blane Lennox will have to go far afield to find what he's looking for. And I can tell you this, I pity the misfortunate girl from the bottom of my heart!'

The girls of Abergour seemed to be rather a thin-skinned lot, Briony was thinking. She had known what it was to have her work criticised. One had to measure up to a job or take the consequences, and she suspected that Annie Skinner was over-fond of the sly cup of tea. Anyway, whether Annie was exaggerating or not, there did not seem to be any other job available in the district. All she could do was to apply for the job and if she was accepted put up with it no matter how awful it might be.

So it was that when at last Annie's flow of gossip had come to a halt, Briony turned not along the street in the direction of Amulree Cottage, but in the opposite direction, and soon found herself once more under that huge sign with its pointing hand. But arrived there, she stood for a few moments hesitating. If all she had heard about Blane Lennox was true then he was rather an ogre—not that that mattered any more, she told herself.

Her interview with Jeremy that morning had done more than open her eyes to his character. It had altered her whole attitude towards men. In future they would find a certain steeliness in her manner, she told herself. From now on she would stand up for her rights and never again give her heart wholly and unreservedly to any man.

She pushed open the gates and walked along the drive. And as she did so she was rehearsing the coming interview. It would be fatal to reveal how inexperienced she was where horses were concerned. It was clear that where Blane Lennox was concerned it did not do to be apologetic and diffident. With this arrogant man a strong, self-confident line would be necessary. To underrate herself would be a great mistake. She would have to speak up for herself if she wanted to secure this job.

She had just come to this decision as she reached the stables. She stopped a tall thin boy who was crossing the yard with a bucket of water in each hand and asked him where she could find Mr Lennox.

'Tack room,' he replied shortly, jerking his head in the direction of what had formerly been the big double garage of Birchfields.

Briony went forward and stood just inside the doorway. How changed it was! The walls were whitewashed. On hooks hung bridles and various pieces of harness. On the stove a bucket of mash was heating. A man stood with his back to her speaking to the boy who had directed her to Amulree Cottage.

'An improvement, but still not good enough!' the man was saying. Swiftly he unfastened the buckles on the girth he was holding in his hand. 'Every single piece of leather must be cleaned separately. And in future use more polish on the buckles. You'll have to do better than this, you know, Johnny, if you want to stay on here.'

Some slight movement on Briony's part, or perhaps the fact that Johnny glanced in her direction, brought to the man's attention the fact that there was someone else present.

He swung around and Briony found herself transfixed by the gaze of a pair of extraordinary blue eyes: they were startlingly bright and penetrating against the deep tan of his skin. And what struck her immediately were the grim and deeply carved lines which marked his face. He was not handsome, she decided. His jaw seemed to jut forward, stiff and arrogant. Of medium height, he was well built, hard and sinewy. He wore a well-worn but beautifully cut hacking jacket. Immediately he gave the impression of a man who would demand instant obedience and who would expect life to conform to his wishes. And it crossed Briony's mind that even if she had not heard so much about him she would have known instantly that this was Blane Lennox.

CHAPTER THREE

'YES? And who might you be?' he enquired, the blue eyes raking her.

Instantly Briony gave up all hope of impressing him by pretending to a greater knowledge of horses than she possessed; she knew instinctively that such a course would prove fatal. Her carefully rehearsed speech fled from her mind. 'I've come about—— I mean, I heard in the village—— I've been told——' To her annoyance she heard herself make stammering attempts to open the conversation.

With determination she threw her head back, drew a deep breath and began again. 'If you're looking for someone to assist in teaching children to ride I'd like to apply for the job.'

Well, at least, she thought, it was short and to the point—even if he did throw her out.

She heard Johnny draw in a little hissing breath as he glanced at her warningly, and for the first time she became aware that her manner was extraordinarily aggressive and defiant.

At the sound Blane Lennox had swung around. 'Very well, Johnny, that will do. Off with you,' he said.

With a look of relief Johnny scuttled away.

Blane Lennox brushed aside a tin of saddle soap and various brushes and leaned against the rough table. 'So that's the latest rumour, is it?' he remarked dryly. 'I must admit it's more innocuous than most of them. Perhaps if you'd heard some of the more lurid gossip you wouldn't have had the nerve enough to venture here.'

Briony stared at him blankly. The interview was not being conducted at all upon the lines she had expected, and she felt at a complete disadvantage. There was something extraordinarily penetrating about the blue gaze, as if he could read her very mind, she thought uneasily. 'I—I heard some talk about it in the village. Of course, if they've got it wrong——'

He ignored this.

'And what have you been doing until now?' The raking glance went to her fingers, white and manicured. They must be a complete giveaway, she thought, and instinctively she put them behind her back.

'Those are not the hands of someone used to working outdoors,' he stated flatly.

No, there was no chance that she could possibly deceive this man, she told herself hopelessly.

'I worked in a firm of accountants,' she told him resignedly.

He raised his thick brows. 'Ideal qualifications for a riding school!'

Her first impulse was to turn away, make a dignified retreat, but she swallowed her pride as she remembered that hideous interview with Jeremy. Anything was better than having to return home ignominiously. 'I had a Shetland pony when I was a child,' she began desperately, 'and later on my father gave me a——'

'So you can ride a Shetland pony—or could ride one when you were a child. But did you muck out, clean harness? What about grooming? I expect you did nothing but ride this animal while someone else did the dirty work!'

He had an extraordinarily brusque way of throwing out his questions that made her hackles rise. How right Hettie had been in everything she had said about him! The man had insufferable manners.

'I took complete charge of "the animal",' she told him. 'My father saw to that. He would let me have Pixie only on condition that I took good care of him, besides——'

'That's all very well and good,' he broke in. 'And although this job is mostly about teaching young children to ride, there's no division of labour here, you know. Everyone has to pitch in just as they're needed. I do it myself and I expect everyone else to do the same.'

'Just a moment,' Briony said, nettled, 'perhaps you'd be good enough to let me know if this job is still open. Perhaps you've already chosen someone?'

'The job is still open *for the right person*,' he replied. 'Can you take care of a spirited horse, exercise it, groom it, feed it—by yourself that is—without expecting Johnny or one of the other boys to come running to your assistance every time it as much as rears?'

Briony hesitated. There was such a temptation to pretend that she could. She wanted the job so badly. And it flashed across her mind that Johnny seemed friendly and would probably help her in the first few days. Perhaps she would be able to get by.

But her hesitation had been fatal. Those strange brilliant blue eyes were fixed upon her with a look of such discernment that she knew instantly that this was just a test question. Already he knew she was incapable of doing this.

'Of course I couldn't,' she replied, her manner as abrupt as his own.

'Well, you're honest at least,' he told her.

'Why shouldn't I be?' she flashed.

'I must say I admire your nerve,' he said. 'To come here applying for a job handling horses when your total experience amounts to caring for a Shetland!'

'Later on I had a New Forest pony,' she informed him. 'But if I don't suit, that's all you have to say. There's no need to be so horribly rude.'

She turned away and was about to leave when he said, 'Just a moment! *I'll* make the decisions here, if you don't mind. It's true you're not suitable. On the other hand, no one who completely fits the bill has turned up. But I may as well warn you here and now that the Lennox Riding School carries no passengers. You'd better pull your weight or I'll know the reason why.'

'You don't think I expect to be paid for nothing?' she retorted. 'I shall certainly give full satisfaction, you may be sure of that!'

But this proud speech did not impress him. 'That's no more than I should expect.'

Briony swallowed, restraining her temper with an effort. 'I take it then that I'm hired?' she asked icily. 'And may I add that I consider——'

But before she could get any further he interrupted, 'Yes, I know what you're going to say—that you consider me abominably rude. Well, I can't say your opinion interests me a lot. But you must understand this clearly, if you're going to work for me I've no intention of altering my manners to suit your refined sensibilities! By the way, where are you staying? We start the day early here. That means you'll have to find lodgings near at hand. One thing I won't tolerate is people straggling in at all hours of the day.'

Briony drew a deep breath. How she would have loved to give him the answer she felt this remark deserved:

'I'm staying at Amulree Cottage in the village,' she told him, 'so I should be able to be here in good time in the mornings.'

And now she saw his expression change. 'So you're staying with Mrs Gillies. You're lodging with her, I take it?'

She was silent for a moment, her heart sinking.

By this time, of course, Hettie's attitude towards him must have come to his ears. If he disliked Hettie as much as she disliked him, then the information that Hettie was her godmother might put paid to her chances.

She plucked up her courage, tilted her chin and said clearly, 'I'm staying as her guest. She's my godmother.'

'And does she know you're applying for this job?'

'No,' she replied shortly.

He gave a bark of laughter that held no amusement. 'I'd be interested to see her face when she discovers I've hired you! That woman has a vendetta against me because I was fool enough to buy her broken-down old house. Not to speak of the grounds, if you could call them that—full of odds and ends of broken old glass-houses and bedraggled shrubs and stumps of apple trees! It's taken me a fortune to level it out and get it into some semblance of order. But then there's no dealing with people like your godmother! What do they call it? Paranoia, I think is the word. They're convinced everyone is doing them down.'

'How dare you speak of Hettie in that fashion!' Briony snapped, her eyes blazing. 'I agree, she doesn't approve of you. And before I met you, I must say I thought she was exaggerating a bit. But now—well, now I've met you I know that every single thing she said is true.'

With an effort she drew to a halt. This, of course, would be the end of everything! But to her amazement he said calmly, 'Well, I must say you get full marks for honesty at any rate. And that's something new in these interviews, I can tell you. I've been handed so much hogwash by so many applicants, both male and female, but you're the first who's spoken the truth—both about your qualifications and about your attitude towards myself.'

But Briony was not placated. 'I don't see that Hettie's attitude towards you should have anything to do with my application!' she snapped. 'This is between you and me.'

'Very well!' Blane Lennox said curtly.

He turned away and began to examine the harness,

and she realised she was being dismissed. Fuming with annoyance, she swung around and marched off down the drive.

Rage carried her along the road on winged feet. Then as she began to simmer down and consider the situation detachedly she realised that, obnoxious as his manners might be, still she had got the job. Just let Mr Blane Lennox be as nasty as he liked! She would learn to become indifferent to anything he might say or do as long as she held it.

But as she drew near Amulree Cottage she was struck by the thought that Hettie would hardly relish the idea that she was going to work for her sworn enemy. How on earth was she going to break the information?

She found her godmother setting the table in a leisurely way with rose-patterned china. 'Did you have a nice walk, dear?' she greeted Briony. 'I'm so glad you came in now. I was just on the point of making tea.' Her voice dwindled as she ambled off into the kitchen. 'We may as well finish the scones I made this morning. And there's some delicious heather honey I got in the village.'

As they took their places at table and Hettie poured, she said, 'I only wish I could keep you with me, Briony. It's so nice having a young face in the house. And I've been so lonely since I lost Roy. Is there any possibility you could stay on for a while?'

Briony instantly seized the opening this gave her, but she decided to be cautious in presenting her news. 'Oh, but I'd love to stay!' she said. 'But if I were to remain for a while I'd need to find something to do. But there doesn't seem to be many jobs around here.'

'No, that's the trouble,' Hettie agreed. 'Certainly nothing to do with the business world. We don't even have a big hotel where you might find something to do—say, work as a receptionist.'

'But I wasn't thinking of anything like that,' Briony

said quickly. 'In fact what I'd like is something more—well, outdoors.'

Hettie looked at her enquiringly. 'But what had you in mind? Girls don't work on the land here, you know. Even if there were anything like that going, it's very exhausting. You'd hardly be fit for it.'

'I wasn't thinking of that,' Briony told her. 'What I had in mind was something to do with riding. I used to love riding. And, as long as Daddy was alive, I always had a pony.'

'Yes, it would be nice if you could ride while you're here,' Hettie said agreeably. 'But after all, it would only be a pastime. It wouldn't be of any financial help.'

'Well, as a matter of fact it occurred to me I might be able to combine the two things. You were telling me some of the children from Laureston School are keen to learn riding. It would be a nice job. I've always got on well with children.'

Hettie put down her cup. 'Just a minute! I thought the children from Laureston School were to be trained by that Lennox fellow?'

'Yes,' Briony tried to sound casual, 'and I believe he's looking for someone suitable to teach the younger ones.'

Hettie sat up straight and stared at her incredulously. 'Do you mean to tell me you would actually take a job with that—*man*?'

At any other time Briony would have smiled at the vehement way Hettie brought out the word, but now she said, 'Oh come, Hettie, beggars can't be choosers. You know I'll be lucky to get a job anywhere.'

'But not with that scoundrel!' Hettie thumped the table with her fist. 'Never, never, never,' her voice rose, 'will anyone from Amulree Cottage work for him!'

'But I've already taken the job,' Briony told her nervously. 'I saw him this afternoon and he's agreed to take me on.'

She glanced apprehensively at her godmother and was

appalled by the change which had come over her
features.

Hettie rose to her feet, her usually mild expression
quite transformed by rage. She pointed to the door. 'I
should very much have liked to have kept you with me,'
she said in a low choked voice, 'but I'm afraid I shall
have to ask you to leave.'

Although Briony had anticipated that Hettie would
be difficult, she had not expected anything as appalling
as this. There was nothing for it, she realised, but to let
Hettie know the real reason for her arrival at Abergour.

'It's beyond my comprehension how you could consider such a thing when you know what the man's like,'
Hettie told her fiercely. 'After all, you have a good job
to go back to, there's no reason why——'

'But that's just it!' Briony interrupted. 'I don't have a
good job any longer. I threw it up before I came North.
Do sit down a moment, Hettie, and let me explain. I
don't know if Mummy mentioned in any of her letters
that I was engaged to a man called Jeremy?'

Reluctantly Hettie sank back into her chair. 'I don't
see what difference that makes, but I think I remember
the name. Your mother told me that, of all your boy-
friends, he was the one she liked best. She said you
seemed likely to marry and settle down.'

'She was right,' Briony told her. 'I did like him best.
In fact, I was completely crazy about him. But I know
now that all the love was on my side. He didn't really
care. He got a very good job in Aberdeen and I chucked
up my job and followed him. I thought, if he felt the
same way as I did, we could get married. But he let me
know right away exactly where I stood. He'd taken up
with an American girl. Her brother's very wealthy—he's
involved in this North Sea oil business—and of course
money is the important thing as far as Jeremy is concerned, and I didn't stand a chance. I know I was a
fool, but that doesn't help matters now.'

Hettie's expression had softened. 'You're not the first girl to throw everything away for love—and you won't be the last!'

'Well, that's one mistake I won't make again,' Briony said bleakly.

'You mustn't let it embitter you,' Hettie urged. 'As time passes you'll take a different view of things, you'll see.'

'No, I don't think so,' Briony said tightly. 'But the fact remains that if you send me away I shall have to go home, and it won't be easy for me to get another job. Mum's not so well off either. Could I not stay with you here, at least for a while? After all, one doesn't have to like one's boss! Not that there's much possibility of my liking Blane Lennox—he's one of the most maddening men I've ever come across.'

'So that's why you wanted to take a job here,' Hettie said reflectively. 'I did get the feeling when you arrived that something had gone badly wrong for you, but I didn't suspect what it was. You know I wouldn't like to put you out, Briony, all the same the thought of you working for that man is almost more than I can endure. No doubt it will give him a great deal of satisfaction to make the work as difficult for you as possible, because he knows how I feel about him. Stay on here as long as you like, Briony, but as soon as you possibly can, try and get another job. Something suitable will turn up, no doubt.'

When Briony had agreed to this, Hettie continued, 'Now why didn't you consult me before you took this step? It's all been so sudden that it's come as a shock to me.'

'Now, Hettie, you know if I'd as much as hinted what I wanted to do you would have forbidden me,' Briony told her.

A faint smile touched Hettie's face. 'I suppose that's true! And I would have been right to do so. But you'll soon discover that for yourself,' she added ominously. 'And don't come looking to me for sympathy, because I've given you plenty of warning.'

'Don't worry,' Briony said airily, relieved that Hettie had accepted the idea, 'I'm not going to let him nettle me. He can be as rude as he likes and I'll remain cool and detached and completely indifferent. I should imagine,' she added, 'that would madden him more than anything else.'

And suddenly they were both laughing.

But later on that evening when Briony had climbed the steep steps to her room, she found no comfort in the crisp linen sheets and the soft downy mattress. The events of the day flashed before her eyes in little pictures. A full moon shone through the open window and in the woods she could hear the soft cry of a night-bird, yet she turned and tossed, remembering Jeremy's eyes, angry and unfriendly as he turned away from her. She had been rejected, like a lovesick and importunate schoolgirl. She had looked on helpless as he had bent his handsome blond head towards the elegant American girl.

When at last the long slow twilight of the north had filled the room with shadows she got up, crossed to the window, and stood there looking out towards Birchfields. Golden light spilled from one of the windows and suddenly there came vividly before her mind the outline of the face of that strange man, Blane Lennox, the square protruding jaw in the brown deeply lined face and those blazing blue eyes. There was a fascination about the harsh, near-ugly features. Jeremy's nearly classically handsome features seemed to blur and fade. They belonged to the past, she realised with startled awareness. In the future belonged Blane Lennox, harsh as a figure carved out of granite.

As she slid between the cool linen sheets she felt bemused and apprehensive. Blane Lennox was now her employer—and also her enemy. Well, he would find in her a worthy adversary, she thought with satisfaction, as she glided into sleep.

She was up early on the following morning and got ready quickly. It was just five minutes to seven as she entered the gates of Birchfields. She had arrived exactly on time, she thought with satisfaction.

When she had walked along the drive she found Blane Lennox in the stable yard, his feet planted in that arrogant possessive manner that she was soon to recognise so well.

'So you're on time!' he remarked.

'But of course!' she replied aloofly. 'I made a point of being exactly on time.'

For a moment the long, deeply-carved mouth tightened. So Blane Lennox was not used to his employees sticking up for themselves, she thought with a little complacent glow. Well, he might as well learn right from the start that he couldn't intimidate her!

Without answering he swung around to speak to a boy over the half door of one of the stables. And as he came out, leading a horse, Briony saw that it was the same tall thin boy who had directed her to the tack room on the previous afternoon. He darted her a quick rather unfriendly glance and was about to move away across the yard when with a slight movement of his hand his employer arrested him.

Blane Lennox turned his attention to Briony again. 'By the way, you didn't tell me your name yesterday. What is it?'

'Briony Walton,' she told him.

'Miss Briony Walton will be working here in future,' he told the boy, 'so you and Johnny had better watch your Ps and Qs.'

The boy's face grew sulky and Briony bit her lip in exasperation. This was just the sort of remark calculated to make the boys antagonistic towards her. Was he testing her out to see if she could stay the course, or had it been no more than one of his usual rough, unthinking remarks? It would be hard to tell.

As the boy led the horse off towards one of the paddocks, Blane Lennox said to r, 'I'm rather surprised to see you here today. I felt sure Mrs Gillies would put her foot down. How did she take the news that you'd decided to work for that ogre Blane Lennox?'

If she had been speaking to any other man, Briony would instinctively have tried to smooth over Hettie's objections. But to him she was determined to make no concessions. 'She wasn't pleased,' she told him flatly. 'She doesn't like my working for you. In fact, she objects very strongly.'

His thick dark eyebrows pulled down in a straight line across his forehead. 'And you don't like working for me either?'

'There was nothing else available.'

'Well, that answers my question, doesn't it? Are you always as forthright as this?'

By admitting this was not so she would be confessing to the chink in her armour and letting him know she was being deliberately defensive. But before she could reply he said thoughtfully, 'Briony—that's an unusual name, but somehow it suits you. And now, Briony, it's time you got to work. As it's your first day you can start off in the tack room. Try to square it up. The boys leave it in an awful mess as a rule. After that you can help water the ponies.' And turning, he strode away.

At least one always knew where one was with Blane Lennox, she thought, a little piqued at the abrupt dismissal.

He was right about the tack room, she decided, as she surveyed it in dismay. Bottles of liniment were scattered among tins of saddle soap and metal polish. On a windowsill was a half empty bottle of milk, some unwashed mugs and the remains of a half-eaten snack. She set to work determinedly. She would let her new employer know right away that she had no intention of slacking.

It didn't take her long to get things shipshape. Finally there remained the snack on the windowsill to be dealt with, and she was wondering what she ought to do with someone's half eaten roll when she became conscious that she was being observed, and turned to find Johnny regarding her, a smile on his freckled face.

'Hello! So you're really working here? This is a bit of luck. First time a pretty girl has joined the gang!' he said with boyish admiration, and Briony had to laugh.

'Thanks! But I doubt if I'll look very pretty by the end of the day. This isn't the sort of job for anyone who wants to look glamorous.'

'No.' He sauntered about admiring the new order she had established. 'I'm sorry, it was a bit of a mess. The boss is always on to us about the way we keep it, but usually when the tack's finished there just isn't time to tidy up.'

'It appears to me that Mr Lennox has very high standards,' Briony sniffed.

Johnny looked at her, faintly puzzled. 'Yes, that's true. But then he works very hard himself, you know.'

'You seem to like working for him,' Briony remarked. 'But from what I've seen so far he appears to be a bit of a taskmaster.'

'He doesn't go in for fancy talk,' Johnny admitted. 'And he has some splendid animals. No broken-down old nags for the Lennox Riding School! I like it here—I always wanted to work with horses. And Mr Lennox's bark is worse than his bite.'

'His bark is quite enough as far as I'm concerned,' Briony told him.

Johnny grinned. 'You don't know half of it. Watch you don't get into hot water or you'll really get the edge of his tongue!'

She glanced about with satisfaction. 'I don't think he

can have any complaints about the tack room at any rate—except for those dreadful bits and pieces on the windowsill.'

'Oh, just shove them in the cupboard,' Johnny told her airily. 'And mind you don't throw away Andy's bun,' he added with a grin. 'He'll want it for his elevenses.'

'And now I'd better give a hand helping to water the ponies,' Briony remarked when she had done as he directed. 'And I think you'd better get back to work or Mr Lennox will be down on you like a ton of bricks.'

Johnny sighed as he slid off the table. 'All right, but I'll help you with the buckets first. They're pretty heavy. I can't imagine why the boss gave you that job.'

Well, I can, Briony was thinking as she walked towards the water trough in the yard. He intended her to realise that unless she could measure up to Johnny and Andy she would not be worth her keep, and he was determined to test her mettle at the outset.

She told Johnny that she would be perfectly well able to manage on her own, but he insisted on helping her with the first bucket. They were half way across the yard when a deep harsh voice startled both of them. Water from the bucket splashed over and drenched Briony's ankles. Johnny turned, blinking nervously as Blane Lennox advanced. His walk was typical of the man, Briony decided, deliberate—yes, and arrogant too.

'I want it to be understood, Johnny, that you're not here to assist Briony. You've your own work to do. Go about it immediately.'

As Johnny hastened away, Briony picked up the bucket. As Johnny had said, it was heavy, but aware that Blane Lennox was watching her, she held herself as upright as possible. She would let him see that she was able to measure up to the boys.

But she breathed a sigh of relief when, later in the

morning, they had a tea-break in the tack room. Andy McLeish quickly returned to work, but Johnny lingered a little.

As he followed her out into the yard, a small car drove in. Out of it stepped a tall slim girl and a child in riding clothes.

'Here comes trouble!' Johnny told her. 'That Sandra Wilson is a little devil. She's here for her own special lesson. Not that she'll ever be able to ride well, not if she kept at it until she's a hundred! But she thinks she knows it all and can't be taught.'

'Is that her mother with her?' Briony asked.

'Not likely!' Johnny laughed. 'That's Senga MacNeil. She's games mistress, or whatever you like to call her, at Laureston School. She's new to the place, and I'll say this for her, she's a great rider, almost as good as the boss, and he's one of the best.'

And now Briony looked at the tall girl more attentively. She was not really very good-looking, her face was rather too long and narrow, but the high cheekbones and slightly slanted eyes gave her an exotic look, and she wore her clothes with style. It was easy to picture her as an athlete, skiing at Aviemore, playing a hard game of tennis, excelling at all outdoor sports.

At this point Blane Lennox made his appearance, and stood chatting with Senga MacNeil while Sandra Wilson, looking bored and sullen, flicked at her shoes with her crop.

A few moments later Blane came striding towards the tack room. 'Ah, there you are!' he exclaimed to Briony. 'I've a pupil for you.'

'What?' Briony exclaimed. 'You mean, give a lesson—now?' She gazed at him in dismay. Somehow she didn't feel ready to give a lesson yet: she had not become acclimatised to this new job. Besides, she had not expected to have to give lessons to children as old as Sandra. She had visualised herself as leading out the very young children. It was rather daunting to have to deal right away with a pupil who, according to Johnny, thought she knew everything already.

But Blane Lennox was saying, 'Yes, a lesson now. Why not? That's what you're employed for, isn't it?'

CHAPTER FOUR

'YES. Yes, of course!' she said quickly.

'Well then, shake a leg,' he commanded impatiently. 'Johnny will saddle up for you. Use the Fells pony and Boru.' He swung around and disappeared.

As she left the tack room with Johnny she saw him rejoin Senga MacNeil. They spoke together for a moment or two and then strolled off towards the house. The girl Sandra wandered off and began prowling about among the stables while Johnny and Briony saddled the ponies.

'Penny is a nice little pony,' Johnny was remarking as he tightened the girths on the Fells pony. 'She's sure-footed and safe. Now Boru's a different cup of tea,' he went on as he placed the saddle on the back of the Connemara pony and slid it back into place. 'Boru is as good as gold in the right hands, but he's lively and has a mind of his own.'

Grateful for the tips, Briony decided that Sandra had better ride Penny, but when all was ready and Johnny had hurried off to his own tasks, it soon became clear that Sandra had other ideas.

'I'm not going to ride that stodgy old Fells pony,' she protested when it was made clear to her that Penny was to be her mount. 'I'm to get lessons in jumping any day now. Besides,' And here she cast Briony a sly glance from the corners of her eyes, 'Mr Lennox said I was to have Boru next time. He said I've come on so well I'm perfectly well able to ride him now.'

Briony hesitated. Sandra's mouth was set in sulky determination and it was clear she was bent upon getting her own way. Was it true, Briony wondered, that Blane

Lennox had said she was sufficiently advanced to ride the lively little Connemara pony? According to Johnny Sandra had no talent for riding, but then his standards were probably pretty high. If only there were someone she could consult! There was no sign now of either Andy or Johnny, and she could not bring herself to go to the house and ask Blane Lennox himself. The thought of the cutting remarks he would make—and in front of the elegant Senga MacNeil too—was enough to make her dismiss the idea immediately.

As she hesitated she became aware that Sandra was watching her, a sly look on her sullen face. If she were to delay any longer she would lose all control of the situation, Briony told herself.

She straightened her shoulders determinedly. 'Very well, you may ride Boru, but I hope for your own sake you're telling the truth. If Mr Lennox said you may ride Boru, then that's all right, but as he isn't here——'

Sandra gave a little crowing burst of laughter. 'No, he's not here. He's probably canoodling with Senga MacNeil and you may be sure he wouldn't want you to interrupt them. She fell for him the very first moment she saw him—it was written all over her face. So you may be sure *she* wouldn't want you to interrupt them either.'

'Come along,' said Briony, breaking in upon this. 'It's time you had your lesson.'

They walked the ponies along the road for a short distance and then Sandra led the way up a narrow sloping path.

Following her, Briony was able to judge her riding ability, and instantly she was struck by the fact that everything Johnny had said about Sandra was correct. The child seemed to have no natural aptitude for riding. She sat her mount awkwardly, like a sack of flour.

When they came to a part where the path widened

out, Briony began to instruct her. 'You're slumping in the saddle,' she told her. 'Hold yourself upright and don't saw on Boru's mouth.'

As Sandra received these instructions she darted Briony a surly glance, then stuck out her lower lip and relapsed into a brooding silence.

It was clear Sandra was the child of rich and indulgent parents who could not deny their lone chick anything her heart desired. And no doubt her pettish behaviour had left her without any friends at Laureston School. Briony went on with the lesson, commenting on the faults she saw in Sandra's riding, and eventually Sandra said furiously, 'I shouldn't be walking along like this, you know. Daddy says I should be jumping by this time.'

Briony gasped. 'Well, you're not going to try jumping—not while you're my pupil! Why, you haven't mastered even the most elementary things about riding.'

'That's not true!' Sandra blazed. 'I *can* jump. I *can* jump!'

Their course had taken them in a wide loop behind the Riding School and they were now about to re-enter the grounds from the opposite side. Briony caught a glimpse of Blane Lennox and Senga MacNeil in the stable yard. They were standing talking, obviously waiting for Sandra's return.

Whether she desired to return in style, or perhaps because she wanted to give the lie to Briony's criticisms, Sandra suddenly urged the Connemara forward, setting it towards a low wall about a couple of feet high.

Seeing how slackly she was sitting in the saddle, Briony cried out, 'Stop! Slow down, Sandra!'

An accident was averted only by the fact that before she reached the wall Sandra slid helplessly sideways from the saddle and fell into a narrow and very muddy burn which ran beside the path. By the time Briony arrived at the spot Sandra was already rising to her feet.

Her cream jodhpurs were now encrusted with mud, her jacket and hair soaked and, to complete the picture, her riding hat was floating like a little boat on the stream, sailing away in the direction of the stables.

Her mishap had knocked all the perkiness out of her. When, with Briony's help, she stood once more on firm ground, she looked dazed and forlorn.

'There, you're all right. You're not hurt,' Briony told her consolingly. She took out her handkerchief and without much success was trying to wipe some of the mud from the girl's jodhpurs as Blane Lennox and Senga MacNeil joined them.

'Look at my new riding clothes!' Sandra wailed. 'What's Mummy going to say?'

'What happened?' Blane Lennox broke in abruptly.

'It was all her fault,' Sandra defended herself. 'She was very rude. She said I was slack in the saddle and that I don't hold the reins properly. She kept nagging and nagging and——'

'Just a moment! Why was the child riding Boru?' he asked Briony.

'She told me you said she was sufficiently advanced to ride the Connemara pony.'

'And you believed her?' he snapped.

'Come, Blane!' Senga MacNeil laid a slim brown hand on his arm. 'Give the girl a chance! She's new here. How was she to know Sandra's a little exhibitionist, always showing off! But come along, Sandra,' she added. 'We'd better be getting back. Although what they're going to think when they see you in that condition, I don't know. Still, I suppose it serves you right, because you'll very definitely be in trouble when we get back to the school.'

But Briony took pity on Sandra, who at that moment looked a picture of misery. She was shivering slightly. Wet and miserable, she was clearly apprehensive of her reception at Laureston. 'Let me take her to the tack room first and give her a cup of tea,' Briony pleaded. 'She could warm up, and maybe I could clean her up a bit.'

'Yes, that's a good idea, especially if you could make her a bit more presentable,' the games mistress said with relief. It was clear she was pleased at Briony's suggestion. 'There would be one of those tiresome inquisitions if she were to return to the school in that condition,' she told Briony.

Briony glanced in Blane Lennox's direction. Frowningly he nodded assent, and immediately she took the child off to the tack room.

As she placed a cup of milky sweet tea in Sandra's hands and rummaged around for a sugary bun with currants left over from the morning break, she was surprised to hear Sandra say, 'I'm sorry I blamed you.' With an effort she added, 'It wasn't your fault I fell off, of course, but——'

'But you had to get yourself off the hook,' Briony finished.

Somehow, although she was aware that the incident might cost her her job, she could not feel any animosity against this lonely misfit of a child.

As colour began to creep back into Sandra's pale cheeks, Briony took out her own comb and began to tease out the tangles in the child's long bright fair hair.

Suddenly, to Briony's astonishment, Sandra laid down the remains of the bun and burst out, 'I *hate* riding!'

'What?'

'I hate it. I hate it!' cried Sandra shrilly. 'I'm so frightened all the time. And Daddy's bought me a beautiful white pony and I won't be able to stay on, and Daddy doesn't know I can't jump, and——'

'Tell me, Sandra,' Briony interrupted, 'did you have a little Shetland pony when you were very small?'

'No, last year is the very first time I ever had a pony.'

'But why was that, if your father wants you to be a good horsewoman?'

'Because when I was tiny we were quite poor. It's only now that we have cars and ponies and a beautiful big house, and I'm able to go to Laureston School.'

'And now you have a pony of your own at home and your father wants you to learn how to ride well? Is that it?'

'Yes. You see, he wants me to join a pony club and ride in gymkhanas. And I want to win prizes so that he'll be proud of me and know what a great horsewoman I am. But I can't help being frightened.'

'Mr Lennox has bought Shetland ponies for the younger children,' Briony remarked. 'Perhaps one of them might suit you and you could go back and begin again from the beginning. You would have far more confidence if you were on a very little pony and felt sure you wouldn't fall off.'

'But Shetland ponies aren't nice—not really,' Sandra complained. 'They bite me and kick me when they get the chance. Anyway, I hate horses,' she added.

'There doesn't seem to be any answer to that,' Briony admitted.

She damped a sponge and removed as much mud as she could from the once immaculate jodhpurs.

As they were about to go out, Sandra said in a small voice, 'You're not the smallest bit afraid of horses, are you?'

'No,' Briony admitted. 'But I think that's because I learned to ride when I was very little. I had a wonderful little Shetland called Pixie. He was mischievous in many ways and sometimes if he was cross with me he used to buck me off. But I didn't mind, because he was so small that I hadn't far to fall. But before that I had a lovely little grey donkey. He was a great pet and I loved him very much.'

'Now donkeys are *nice*. I wish I had a donkey,' Sandra

said wistfully. 'They're so cuddly and they walk along very slowly and you don't have to worry in case you fall off. Only I suppose I'm too tall now.'

'It would depend on what size the donkey was,' Briony told her. 'On the Continent, grown-up people ride on donkeys and nobody thinks it's the least bit strange.'

They went across the yard and joined Blane and Senga, who were standing chatting near Senga's small neat car.

Senga surveyed Sandra critically. 'Well, you have done wonders!' she congratulated Briony. 'She's quite presentable now—well, at least, passable.' She smiled. 'I'll be able to smuggle her into the school without creating too much of a scene.' To Sandra she said, 'We'll keep this little adventure to ourselves, if you like. There's no need for us to spread it about the school. After all, everyone falls off when they're learning to ride and—to say the least of it—you're no exception.'

At this Sandra brightened and gave a rather watery smile.

Sandra seated herself in the car and Briony moved away across the yard and as she did so she heard Senga say, 'I'll be along for my own lesson tomorrow. You'll let me have the palomino, won't you?'

'Why the palomino?'

Senga shrugged. 'He jumps well.'

Inside one of the stables Briony could still hear their voices.

'It wouldn't be because you know you look well on a golden horse, would it?' He sounded amused, almost indulgent.

What would Senga reply to this? Briony wondered. By slightly raising her head she could see over the half door. The temptation to steal a peep was irresistible.

Senga's mouth, that was just a little too wide for

beauty, curved into a smile that tilted those exotic, slightly Oriental eyes.

Yes, Senga was definitely very attractive, Briony thought grudgingly, and she was well aware of the effect that generous mouth could have on a man.

'But of course,' she replied airily, as she slid behind the wheel. 'And what's more, I'll probably turn up in eighteenth-century riding clothes—all flowing velvet skirts and natty tricorn hat with feathers sweeping on to my velvet collar. I imagine I'll look quite devastating and give Johnny and Andy a thrill.'

'Don't you dare!' Blane told her. 'They're troublesome enough as it is, and I am particularly susceptible.'

Briony could hear Senga's laughter and saw how, as the car drove off, Blane stood looking after it for a moment or two. What was his expression? she wondered, but his head was turned away from her and it struck her that she would never know.

A moment later and he had crossed the yard with a few strides, and as she met the full impact of those startlingly blue eyes she knew she was in for a stormy session. 'Well, and what have you to say for yourself?' he demanded.

'Say? About—about what?' She despised herself for the quiver in her voice.

'About this mishap to Sandra, of course,' he replied brusquely. 'It wouldn't have happened if you had used your own judgment and kept control of this situation. You're not here to take your instructions from a child like Sandra. You can't teach children properly if you don't let them know who's boss. If you're going to be all soft and sloppy you're not going to be much use here when you have a number of children to control at once.'

Briony bit her lip. This was totally unfair. Quickly she turned her head away, fearing he would see the tears that had sprung to her eyes.

But nothing escaped those penetrating eyes of his. 'Now don't dissolve into floods of tears the first time you're spoken to in a straightforward manner. I speak out straight from the shoulder. That's my way and I've no intention of altering it. If you consider me rude then I'm rude, and you can put up with it or leave. Take your choice!'

It flashed through Briony's mind that being spoken to in this way would, at one time, have reduced her to the tears he so much despised. But now they aroused all her fighting spirit. Steel had entered her spirit at that moment when Jeremy had flung her off so contemptuously.

She squared her shoulders, swung around and faced him, her voice resolute and clear. 'You may be sure there'll be no floods of tears. Anything you care to dish out, I shall be able to take—yes, and more!'

But she did not dare to say anything more. She flung down the pitchfork she had been using and marched out of the stable.

Lunchtime came and she found that this meal was taken in the big kitchen of the house—a kitchen she hardly recognised. It was completely different from the days when Hettie had presided there. Now the flower-pots on the windowsills had disappeared, and the gaily patterned curtains. The room was strictly functional with plenty of clear space and white enamelled cup-boards and a big plastic-topped table with a sturdy work-surface.

Blane lunched with them. He sat at the top of the table, contributing hardly anything to the conversation, as though in an abstracted mood. But she had the feeling that the atmosphere would have been less restrained without his presence.

The meal was served by his housekeeper, Mrs McPhee. She went about her duties silently and gave the impression of being a woman who would hate to indulge in idle gossip.

The boys' subdued conversation formed a background to Briony's thoughts as she reviewed the disastrous ending to Sandra's lesson. Perhaps a donkey would be the answer to the child's problems, she thought with growing enthusiasm. Then, by easy stages, she could be induced to ride a pony with confidence. But how to get a donkey for the child? Under her lowered lashes she studied Blane Lennox covertly. He showed no signs of being in a receptive mood should she approach him about investing in a donkey. He would hardly sympathise with Sandra's dilemma, or understand it.

During the afternoon she was kept busy, but when at last everything was shipshape she decided to take the bull by the horns.

Instead of returning to Amulree Cottage immediately, she paused to run a comb through her hair and to apply a touch of lipstick. Somehow she felt that it was important that she should present a tidy appearance if she was to hope for any success when she explained to him how necessary it was that Sandra should be treated like a special case, and how her aversion to riding could be overcome by a sympathetic and tactful approach.

The boys had disappeared, their day's labours over. Blane had disappeared into the house. Now Birchfields had a deserted and lonely look and as she approached the house her enthusiasm began to wane, and trepidation set in. But, squaring her shoulders, she marched up to the door.

Mrs McPhee showed her into a room which she called 'the study'—a room which was changed beyond recognition from the days when Hettie had been mistress at Birchfields! Then the small low-ceilinged room had been considered her own special sitting-room. Now there was no sign of the embroidered cushions and the cretonne loose covers on the sagging old furniture.

Instead there was a totally masculine atmosphere. The walls were panelled in wood which had a rich dark red glow. Two sides of the room were lined with bookshelves and topped by ranks of silver trophies. The floor was no longer covered by Hettie's patterned carpet. Instead gleamed dark polished wood on which lay sheepskin rugs.

As Mrs McPhee showed Briony in Blane was seated at a broad table engrossed in a pile of forms. 'Oh, it's you,' he remarked. He went to a pipe-rack, gesturing as he did so towards one of the buttoned leather armchairs which stood before the flaming wood fire. 'And what can I do for you?'

Briony gulped and felt her courage oozing away as he filled his pipe and took the chair opposite her. 'It's about Sandra,' she began.

'Do you mind?' he indicated his filled pipe. 'I think I've heard just about enough of that child for the day,' he frowned as he lit up. 'Frankly, I've given her up as a bad job. In fact she's becoming an infernal nuisance.'

'That's just what I want to speak to you about!' She leaned forward eagerly. 'She was telling me today that she's begun to ride only lately. She's terrified of horses, it seems, yet her father insists that she learn to ride. She's never really had a chance to build up confidence, and easily loses courage.'

'Just as I thought! She's a cowardly little thing in spite of all her bragging and showing off.'

'Oh no, she's not cowardly,' she interrupted impulsively. 'Sandra has lots of grit. But she didn't begin learning when she was tiny. I've been thinking that if she could begin again—on a donkey this time—as I did myself, then she would gain confidence.'

He looked at her in astonishment. 'My dear girl, what are you talking about? Why, only a few days ago she was asking me when she could learn to jump.'

'That's because she wants to please her father—although she's scared stiff most of the time.'

Blane sighed and looked at her in exasperation. 'And what is all this leading up to?'

'Just what I said! Sandra needs to begin again—perhaps on a donkey. I'm sure she would come on wonderfully.'

'And you, of course, would be the wonder worker! In no time at all Sandra would be jumping in the Olympics, and you'd get all the credit!'

Briony clenched her fists tightly. How insufferable the man was! she thought indignantly. But at the same time she could feel herself redden. Had she really been hoping that if she made a success of teaching Sandra she would be able to establish herself in his good books?

Then came the familiar wave of exasperation that she always seemed to feel in his presence. How she longed to march out of Birchfields, and out of his life for ever!

He paused for a moment, regarding her. 'So it boils down to this, what you're really asking is that I should buy a donkey. Do you really think I'm going to have a moke wandering about Birchfields, just because you want to prove a point? Well, let me tell you, my dear girl, as far as Sandra's concerned, it's too late to turn the clock back. The wretched child's never going to be any good and the sooner she removes herself the better I'm going to like it. No, I'm afraid you can put the whole idea out of your head. The Lennox Riding School can supply almost any type of horse, but we do not stock donkeys, I'm afraid.'

'Well, it's time you did,' she blurted out, completely forgetting the tactful little speech she had prepared.

She had the satisfaction of seeing that this remark had riveted his attention.

'It amazes me you were ever able to hold a job down if you spoke to your employer in that fashion.'

'But you're not being *reasonable*,' she protested.

'Whether I'm being reasonable or not is none of your business!' His voice had an edge to it. 'If Sandra is having difficulties because her father is pushing her beyond her capabilities, then that's her problem—and his. Let her go to her father and talk it over with him. Perhaps he'll get her a donkey,' he added dryly.

'But she can't do that!' she protested. 'She wants him to be proud of her. How can she possibly admit to him that after all the lessons she has had she's only fit to begin again at the beginning. I must say I gathered from the way she spoke of him that he's a bit of a dragon.'

'Like me, in other words! Is that what you're saying?' His blue eyes gazed at her steadily.

She glanced away, embarrassed. 'I didn't say you were,' she replied rather weakly.

'Come now, don't give me that stuff! The villagers have been letting off steam about me, haven't they? I'm not exactly a favourite around these parts, as no doubt you've heard. And I must say it seems to me your attitude agrees pretty closely with theirs. Not that it matters to me—as long as you do your job properly it doesn't concern me whether you approve of me or not!' He glanced at his watch. 'We've both had a pretty busy day and I suggest we drop the subject. I'm sure you'd like to get home, and I admit I'd like to knock off for a bit.'

Briony felt the colour rise to her face. So she was being summarily dismissed! Her importunities on Sandra's behalf had only bored and exasperated him. If only she had departed as soon as she had seen her mission was a failure! She might have known that once Blane Lennox had made up his mind he was immovable.

'I'm sorry to have wasted your time,' she told him stiffly, as she walked swiftly towards the door.

'Just a minute!' he detained her. 'I haven't finished, you know.'

She turned, waiting resentfully.

'There's just one thing more, Briony. I have the notion—I may be wrong, of course—that you have the feeing that if you work long enough on me you'll get me to reverse my decision. If I ever do change my mind it won't be because of the wiles of a woman, so don't ever bring up this donkey business again. And now, if you've got that straight, off you go.'

CHAPTER FIVE

On the following morning Briony found that the young children from the school were expected for a lesson and she was kept busy preparing the Shetland ponies. One of them, a new arrival at the Riding School, was a delightful little creature with a flowing black mane and tail. But he had not settled down yet and as she went into the paddock and approached him he laid back his ears and showed the whites of his eyes. Briony sighed as she trudged through the damp grass. She was going to have trouble getting a halter on him and bringing him in.

Eventually she pinned him in a corner of the paddock, rushed forward, halter in hand, only to have to jump aside in the nick of time as he lashed out with his heels.

At the same time a voice, none too gentle, called out, 'What do you mean by approaching a Shetland in that fashion? It's a wonder you haven't had a nasty accident!'

Turning, she found Blane Lennox leaning on the rail, the ice-blue eyes regarding her with anything but an amiable expression.

'You should have spoken to him as you came up from behind. Remember it's natural to these animals to run wild in herds, and they're suspicious of anything stealing up on them silently. It denotes danger. Now begin again. Go forward, speaking soothingly, and you'll do a lot better.'

She nodded mutely and followed his instructions, finding it easy now to slip on the halter.

Blane joined her as she led the pony through the gate of the paddock.

'He's a lovely little animal,' she said awkwardly, finding that he was striding along beside her in silence.

'Yes, I think Black Prince is going to be quite an asset to the Lennox Riding School—especially for the very young kids.' For a moment he glanced at her briefly. 'I gather you haven't ridden much since you were a child.'

Briony shook her head. 'After Daddy died my mother and I weren't very well off. It would have been impossible for us to keep a pony. Anyway, I had to take a job in an office and wouldn't have had time to take care of it properly.'

'I see! And did you like this office job?'

'No, I prefer outdoor work. Anything to do with horses is ideal as far as I'm concerned.'

'Then there was no stables or riding school nearby where you could have got employment, is that it?'

'Well, yes, there was a place fairly near,' she replied reluctantly.

'But that would have been ideal, wouldn't it?'

'Yes, I suppose so!'

'Yet you didn't take up something nearer home. You've come quite a long way to end up working in the Lennox Riding School.'

She hesitated, wary of what the next question might be. Blane Lennox was the last person in the world she would want to know her reason for travelling so far from home.

'I—I was—was visiting my godmother,' she began stammeringly. 'And—and when I heard of the job I thought it might be fun. Something different, you understand.'

'Indeed!' There could be no mistaking the sardonic undertones.

She felt colour flare in her cheeks. It was as though

those strangely penetrating eyes could read her thoughts.

But luckily they had reached the stable yard, and she was able to set to work grooming Black Prince.

Johnny, she found, was brushing a beautiful palomino horse as if his very life depended on bringing up the gleam in its golden coat. With every sweep of the body brush the animal looked more like a work of art carried out in molten gold.

Seeing Johnny's efforts, Briony was determined to make Black Prince look as presentable as possible. He had his silken summer coat and it struck her that with a bit of effort on her part she could make the little pony look as beautiful in his own way as the mighty palomino.

She had almost completed her work when Senga MacNeil drove up in a station-wagon that appeared to be bursting at the seams with chattering youngsters. She got out looking superb in well-cut but informal clothes. She wore slacks tucked into boots and a well-cut hacking jacket.

As the children piled out she paused to admire Black Prince. 'You're making a wonderful job of the little Shetland,' she said. 'One so often sees them in their double winter coat, it's easy to forget how pretty they can look.'

While she was speaking Johnny approached her leading the palomino.

With its snowy mane and tail against its golden coat it made an exquisite picture.

'Well, Johnny, you've certainly got Golden Sovereign looking his best!' With a little wave of her hand she said to Briony, 'I won't delay you,' and with Johnny leading Golden Sovereign she went off towards one of the paddocks where jumps had been erected.

From where she stood Briony had a clear view as Johnny helped Senga to mount and as she saw how

Senga sat her horse she knew immediately that Senga was a superb horsewoman.

Shortly afterwards Blane joined her, and Briony turned away as he began to school her in the jumps.

Briony's first task was to establish some sort of order among the excited children. And when she had the children seated on what seemed to her the most suitable mounts she became engrossed in the lesson.

To Briony's surprise Sandra also had turned up. But she made no effort to mount the pony Andy saddled for her. Instead she seated herself upon the topmost rail of the paddock in which the Shetlands were circling and surveyed her little schoolmates scowlingly.

For a moment Briony hesitated. She was anxious to help Sandra, but she felt immediately that there would be no point in trying to get her to join the younger children. No doubt Sandra was simply trying to attract notice in an attempt to bolster her self-confidence.

Time passed quickly. Then she heard Senga call out, 'That's enough, children! It's time we were getting back to school.'

And Briony found that Senga and Blane were watching her. How long had they been there? she wondered. And what faults had Blane picked up? He certainly would give her no praise for her efforts, she felt sure. Oh well, she would soon hear all about it, she was thinking as she lifted the tiniest children from their saddles and led them back into the yard.

As the children piled into the station-wagon, chattering excitedly, Senga said to Briony, 'I don't know how you've the patience! Some of the children can be so troublesome. And then there's Sandra—she's a handful. I don't know how you put up with her.'

She slipped behind the wheel and with a wave of her hand drove along the drive.

As Briony moved away she saw Blane approaching,

hands in pockets, staring thoughtfully at the ground.
She quickened her steps, anxious to reach the tack room
before he could waylay her. But it was as though he had
anticipated this move.

'Just a minute, Briony! I've something to say to
you.'

She stopped with a sigh, feeling tired and dispirited.
He had not stopped her to heap her with words of
praise, of that she felt sure. 'Well, what have I done
wrong now?' she demanded, taking the bull by the
horns.

He frowned thoughtfully, pausing before answering—
just long enough to make her feel vaguely uncomfortable.

'I don't intend to reproach you. As far as I could see
the lesson went pretty satisfactorily.'

'Pretty satisfactorily!' she thought acidly. How typi-
cally grudging of the man. His eyes were meeting hers
challengingly and she determined not to let herself
become intimidated. 'Well, you nearly always do find
something wrong!'

'Do I indeed?' And to her surprise she thought she
heard faint amusement in his voice. 'What a temper
we're in! It seems to me that a hot cup of tea might
improve the situation. But before you go—I've been
watching that Sandra kid and I've decided that the best
thing would be for you to tell her the next time she
turns up that it's all over. She's nothing but a bad influence. Before we know where we are the rest of the
urchins will be throwing tantrums. Yes, I'm afraid her
daddy is wasting his money on that kid, and the sooner
it's brought home to him the better.'

Briony stared at him in stupefaction. 'You mean, you
want *me* to tell her not to come again?'

'That's exactly what I mean.'

'But why me?' she asked, aghast.

'Because you're her teacher, of course. She's one of

your pupils, isn't she? It's obvious she's never going to make a rider. And a dud like that won't do the reputation of the Lennox Riding School any good. It's clear her father is a man who thinks success is very important. As soon as he discovers how little Sandra has learned he'll be sure to spread it about that the Lennox Riding School is not up to its job.'

'But I couldn't possibly tell Sandra not to return,' she gasped.

'And why not, may I ask? Don't you agree that she's making no real effort to learn?'

'No, I don't,' she said hotly. 'Sandra's main trouble is that she's afraid. I told you that, but you don't listen to me.'

He gave a sigh of exasperation. 'Don't tell me you're bringing up this donkey subject again!'

'No! And I certainly don't intend to,' she told him. 'All I hope for now is that she'll become acclimatised and ease into things gradually.'

'Well, she's not going to acclimatise herself at my riding school,' he told her bluntly. 'I don't believe in experiments of that sort! It's time Sandra realised that we don't want any little show-off around here. The sooner she clears off the better. So you'd better have a cup of tea and think over what I've said.'

And before she could think of a suitable rejoinder, he turned on his heel and walked swiftly away.

The manners of the man! Briony thought furiously as she went towards the tack room. So she was expected to do his dirty work for him! Well, she'd show him! So he thought she should have a nice cup of tea and think things over! It would take more than a cup of tea to extinguish the flaming temper she felt!

She found Johnny putting on the kettle. He looked curiously at her for a moment. 'Dear me, your cheeks *are* red—but nicely so,' he added hastily.

'Thanks,' Briony said dryly. 'It wouldn't surprise me

at all if I was purple in the face! That Blane Lennox is one of the most objectionable and rude people I've ever come across in my life!'

He turned from the stove. 'You mean he ticked you off?'

'I should say so, and in no uncertain terms! Would you believe it, he wants *me* to get rid of Sandra!'

'Well, she is a bit of a nuisance, isn't she?' he replied. 'I mean, there's no end to the mischief she can get up to when she's in the mood.'

'You sound as if you're siding with him,' she said angrily.

'Well, Sandra's not getting anywhere,' he replied. 'And she'll only encourage the other children to get out of hand too, if she can get away with her nonsense. The fact is that Mr Lennox is very fair. Oh, I admit he can be sharpish at times, but he'll never tick you off in front of anyone else and make you feel small. And then he's as straight as a die when it comes to business. I've never seen the smallest sign of crookedness in him.'

'You're certainly giving him a good character,' Briony retorted acidly.

Johnny reached down some mugs and began to butter some buns. 'Why shouldn't I? He's always been decent enough to me. And once when a stallion threw me and injured me, he saw I had the best treatment. He used to visit me in hospital and drop in on my mum every time he passed the house.'

Briony maintained a morose silence as Johnny poured boiling water into the teapot.

He glanced at her over his shoulder, his freckled face split with a grin. 'Here, have a bun and a nice strong mug of tea and you'll feel better! In fact, I shouldn't be surprised if you came to like the boss as time rolls by!'

'Like him?' she repeated disbelievingly. 'I can't stand

the man. He's completely unendurable. I simply loathe him,' she declared emphatically.

Johnny poured a mug of tea and offered her a plate of iced buns. 'Well, all I can say is that you're an exception. Most women fall for him hook, line and sinker. Not that he's particularly handsome,' he added with an air of impartiality.

'I should say not!' Briony returned. 'And besides that, he's one of the most unlikeable people I've ever come across!'

'Well, Senga MacNeil doesn't think that,' Johnny told her with a sly look.

'You mean she's in love with him?' Briony asked doubtfully.

'Of course! Everyone knows that.' Even Andy, and he's not particularly observant.'

'Who's not particularly observant?' Andy enquired as he wandered in and claimed his mug of tea.

'You,' Johnny told him. 'I was telling Briony that even you spotted that Senga's fallen for the boss.'

'So she has,' Andy agreed. 'Anyone can see that.'

'I can't,' Briony protested.

'But you haven't been here very long. Watch out and you can't help spotting it.'

'Then she must have rotten taste!' Briony exclaimed.

Andy chewed on a bun. 'I imagine he's got what's called charm. And the ladies prefer that to good looks any day, if you ask me.'

'Huh!' Briony scoffed. 'I just can't believe that a wonderful girl like Senga MacNeil could fall for a man like him.'

'Don't let's bother about him any more,' Johnny pleaded. 'What about coming down to the café for a cup of coffee this evening when we knock off? You can forget all about the boss for a while.'

'That's Johnny's usual approach,' Andy warned. 'As soon as he sees a pretty girl he invites her to coffee and cream cakes and expects her to fall into his arms.'

'I'll settle for coffee and cream cakes,' Briony said, laughing.

'Good! Give me time to change into my best bib and tucker and I'll meet you outside Amulree Cottage,' Johnny told her.

The thought of having some time off that evening made Briony's spirits rise. Often Hettie would wear a faintly disapproving expression, showing Briony that she was resentful that she was working for her arch enemy. Sometimes Briony would go to her room early to avoid her godmother's silent disapproval.

But that evening when she had changed into a floral-patterned dress she found Johnny waiting for her, his face eager and shining from a generous application of soap and water.

He glanced at her in open admiration. 'You look even prettier in that dress! Don't ever wear jeans again.'

She laughed as she accompanied him along the village street. 'I can just imagine what I'd look like after mucking out a stable!'

Still, she had to admit to herself that young and immature as Johnny was, there was something very gratifying about his open boyish admiration. It would be hard to imagine Blane Lennox even handing out such compliments. She giggled at the very idea.

'Here we are!' Johnny remarked as they came to an attractive-looking cottage with 'Teas' written outside in large letters. They went in through the invitingly open door to find themselves in a large room spotlessly clean and humming with the buzz of holidaymakers.

Johnny ordered importantly. 'The cream cakes are really super here,' he told her. 'I can especially recommend the éclairs. By the way, I've got a secret about the boss!' As the cream cakes arrived he leaned over conspiratorially. 'But you must swear not to let him know I told you.'

Briony opened her eyes wide, anticipating some particularly interesting piece of gossip.

'You'll never guess what he's going to do!'

She shook her head, mystified.

'It seems a local farmer is advertising a donkey for sale and he's sending me along tomorrow to collect it. I wonder what on earth he wants it for. It's not a bit like him, you know. A donkey would be about the last thing in the world I could imagine him keeping at Birchfields. But remember, don't say I told you, because he hates being talked about.'

'I shan't tell him,' Briony promised with a thrill of excitement. 'Could it be that, after all, he had backed down and actually decided that a donkey could be the answer to Sandra's problems! But when she considered it, she dismissed the idea from her mind. Only that afternoon he had asked her to tell Sandra not to return for further lessons. No, he must be purchasing it for a friend perhaps, who would collect it later. In the meantime he would permit it to graze at Birchfields.

She gave a little sigh. To expect Blane to capitulate was simply wishful thinking. He was not the sort of man to be deflected from a course once he had made up his mind.

'Here, have another cake.' Johnny proffered the plate. 'You're looking down in the dumps again! Why don't you put the boss and his ways out of your mind and enjoy yourself?'

Johnny's advice was good, Briony told herself. All the same, Blane Lennox was not a man whom it was easy to dismiss from one's thoughts.

Before they parted Johnny told her that the donkey was to be collected within the next few days. The arrangement was that he was to take it to the Riding School in a horse box from the hill farm.

A few mornings later when Senga drove into the yard in the station-wagon she brought with her not only the usual crowd of excited young children, but also Sandra, and as Briony saw her get out her spirits sank. Sandra would have to be told that she was no longer welcome. If only she could put it off, she thought desperately. But Blane had fixed her with a steady gaze which carried the unmistakable message that he was waiting for her to carry out his instructions.

Reluctantly she approached Sandra, who was again showing signs that she intended to spend her lesson time perched on the rails watching the younger children.

Briony moved slowly, dragging her feet, and was near Sandra when Blane overtook her. She turned. 'It's all right,' she told him coldly. 'I'm going to tell the kid you don't want her.'

He led her back a little. 'Not so fast, young woman,' he said brusquely. 'You'll find a donkey in the end stable. And now it's up to you. The kid can make a kirk or a mill of it, just as she pleases.'

When Briony told Sandra the news, the child followed her excitedly, followed by a chattering group of the younger children. Even the sophisticated Senga joined the procession.

When they reached the stable Briony unbolted the door and a shaft of sunlight lit up the interior. For a moment there was a silence followed by delighted admiration, for standing in the fresh straw was a blue-grey donkey with a thick rich coat and a quaint long-lashed look that was completely irresistible.

'Why, he's just like a dear little teddy-bear!' exclaimed Sandra excitedly, as she unbolted the lower half of the door and rushing in flung her arms around its neck. 'He's so soft, he's like velvet. How I'd love to ride him!'

'That's what he's here for,' Briony told her smilingly. 'Mr Lennox bought him so that you could learn to ride without feeling frightened.'

'Oh, how I love him!' Sandra exclaimed. And Briony was stunned to see that her face, lit by enthusiasm, had lost its sullen hangdog look.

'Yes, it is a pretty little thing,' Senga's cool voice could be heard saying. 'But really, dear, don't you think you're just a little bit too grown-up for that sort of thing? When I rode donkeys it was at the seaside, and I was only a tot. I mean, you don't want people to laugh at you, do you?'

Briony listened in incredulous silence. Sandra's face had fallen and her brows were knitting ominously. 'No, I suppose people would laugh at me. All the same, it is a dear little donkey.'

Why had Senga been so contemptuous and cutting in her remarks? Briony wondered. And for a moment the thought crossed her mind that it had been done deliberately. Senga didn't want Sandra to be successful. And if Sandra refused to ride the little animal it would quickly be sold. It was not Blane's practice to keep useless pets, of that she felt sure.

'Come along, children!' Senga commanded, her voice high and authoritative. 'It's time Miss Walton gave you your lessons.' She clapped her hands to ensure attention and then led the way back to the yard.

The children followed her, with the exception of Sandra, who stood rooted to the spot looking disconsolate.

'Miss MacNeil is right, I suppose, but I would dearly like to have him for my very own.'

'You could, you know,' Briony told her bracingly. 'I told you how grown-ups ride donkeys abroad. When I was in Greece for my holidays I often saw grown-up women riding along on donkeys. They're very strong, you know, and besides a human being they can carry baskets as well. You mustn't feel that you're doing anything extraordinary.'

Sandra looked at her doubtfully. 'Do you really think so?'

'Of course I do!'

'Well, if you say so, I'll have a go!'

'That's a good idea. And even if you do slide off the ground's very near,' Briony told her with a smile.

'That's true,' Sandra agreed happily, and flung her arms around Briony's neck and kissed her swiftly on the cheek.

CHAPTER SIX

DURING the weeks that followed the arrival of the donkey Briony noticed a distinct change in Sandra's attitude towards her riding lessons.

First of all there was the excitement of choosing a name for the latest acquisition to the Birchfields stables. Briony found herself constantly being waylaid by Sandra, who had thought up the most bizarre suggestions. But, much to Briony's relief, she finally decided that 'Teddy' would be the most suitable name.

Now when the station-wagon arrived from Laureston School Sandra was the first to bounce out. She no longer showed scornful rejection of her young companions, but hurried to saddle Teddy, who would be watching eagerly, his furry ears twitching, as soon as he heard the car drive into the stable yard. Now, instead of taking her perch on the paddock rails and frowningly watching the other pupils on their ponies as they circled Briony, Sandra actually joined in, listening attentively as Briony called out her instructions.

Briony tried to stimulate Sandra's interest by giving her special attention at the end of each lesson. One morning, when the other pupils had returned to the stable yard and only Sandra on Teddy was left in the paddock, she felt a little glow of satisfaction as she saw how greatly improved Sandra was. This was followed by a surge of triumph as she spotted Blane approaching on his magnificent black Hanoverian horse. He sat his mount magnificently, she noticed—like a warrior from ancient times.

'Well, are you satisfied?' There was a little ironic quirk

at the corner of his jutting lower lip, as he reined in beside her.

'Satisfied?' she queried with assumed puzzlement.

'Don't pretend you don't know what I mean!'

'Oh, you mean about Teddy?'

He raised his eyebrows enquiringly. 'Teddy? Is that what Sandra calls the moke?'

'Yes, she gave him a name right away, and I think that's a good sign. She seems happy enough. But there's one thing I don't understand.'

'And what may that be?'

'You sounded so adamant about not having a donkey at Birchfields, and I don't think you're the kind of man who changes his mind, so naturally I'm surprised that you've given way, when——'

'Don't flatter yourself!' he broke in. 'I didn't succumb to your wheedlings, if that's what you think. It just so happened that a farmer friend of mine wants to buy a donkey for his children. At the moment they're rather too young to ride it, so when I heard there was one for sale I told him I might be able to use it here at the Riding School for a while and let him have it later. You see, it occurred to me I might as well put your theories to the test. At the moment you seem to be succeeding. All the same, I shouldn't be too optimistic if I were you! It may be the novelty of the thing that appeals to the child at the moment. No doubt when she becomes bored she'll throw the poor old moke over.'

Briony shook her head. 'I don't think so,' she said confidently. 'I'm perfectly certain she's on the right lines.'

Blane looked at her mockingly for a long moment. 'Has anyone ever told you you're extremely self-opinionated?'

'Self-opinionated?' she repeated, genuinely surprised. 'No, and I don't think I am. In fact, I'm the direct opposite!'

'Then you think wrong! It would serve you right if Teddy and Sandra between them took you down a peg or two!'

Before she could make up her mind whether he was serious or not, she noticed Senga strolling towards them.

How was it, Briony wondered, that at times Senga could look beautiful and on other occasions could appear almost plain? This morning she was looking her very best. The crispness of the air had tinted her high cheekbones with the faintest hint of pink, and, as usual, her clothes were excellently tailored.

'Really, Blane,' she began, her eyes on Sandra, who was walking the donkey about the paddock, 'it was completely ridiculous to get a donkey for the child! Giving in to her will only make her more self-willed, and goodness knows, she's a big enough show-off as it is. If you could only realise how troublesome she is at school! Dear old Miss Anderson is quite in despair. I think the only reason she doesn't chuck her out is because Sandra's daddy is so rich,' she added derisively. 'By the way, speaking of my revered headmistress, she mentioned that she'd like us to do some pony-trekking. "The country about Abergour is *so* beautiful, don't you think, Miss MacNeil?" I'd say she thinks it would be a good advertisement for the school.'

'Pony-trekking? The children are hardly advanced enough for that,' he replied.

'Exactly what I was thinking,' Senga agreed. 'But it occurred to me that a treasure hunt might fill the bill. I used to enjoy them so much when I was a kid. Did you, Briony?'

Briony shook her head. 'I never went on a treasure hunt. I remember I took part in a gymkhana when I was quite small. I was very proud when I won the egg-and-spoon race.'

'Yes, a gymkhana can be fun,' Senga agreed, 'but I

must say I always enjoyed treasure hunts more. I remember how madly excited we used to feel when we'd deciphered a clue.'

'Do you know, that's rather a good idea,' Blane told her. 'And more interesting for kids of their age than trekking. We must think it over.'

He wheeled his horse and Senga walked away beside him, her face uplifted towards his, as they discussed this new project.

Left to herself, Briony felt a vague sense of disappointment. How quickly he had lost interest in her and her achievement in teaching the children!

For the next few days he made no reference to Senga's suggestion and Briony wondered if he had given up the idea. But it was hard to tell with this complex employer of hers. And that sardonic face of his gave little away.

She had discovered that, as far as the work was concerned, it did not do to be lulled into a state of false security. It was at moments when she felt most complacent about her achievements that those strange steely blue eyes would flash most intimidatingly. Often, too, it was about some small omission; something a less watchful person than Blane would probably have overlooked. But then he wasn't in the habit of turning the blind eye, even to the smallest mistake, especially when it was a matter of the welfare of the animals.

During the previous week when she was approaching a loose-box carrying a bucket of bran mash for a pony which had caught a chill, he had suddenly appeared from nowhere and had plunged his hand into the bucket and felt the temperature of the mash. 'Too hot!' he announced brusquely.

'I—I thought it would be all right—by the time I'd carried it across the yard, I mean,' Briony had muttered.

'Well, you thought wrong!' he had told her curtly. 'And may I remind you that *I* make the decisions at

Birchfields. Simply carry out my orders without any arguments.' And without another word he had turned away, leaving her fuming.

This was why, when one evening, just as she was about to leave for Amulree Cottage, she was told she was wanted in the study by the boss—as the boys usually called their employer—she felt vaguely uneasy.

During the day he had shown no sign that she was in his black books—but then, who could tell?

As Mrs McPhee showed her into the study she hoped fervently that she didn't look as nervous as she felt. This time, she told herself, she would show some backbone and not stand giving weak, inept excuses for whatever transgressions Blane accused her of.

She tilted back her head and straightened herself resolutely as she stepped into the room. 'You sent for me,' she began, very much on her dignity.

But the effect was marred by the fact that he was standing with his back to her by one of the windows studying a large map which was spread out on a low oak table.

For a moment he continued rocking on his heels as though lost in thought, but when he turned he appeared completely affable. He waved her to a chair. 'First of all I want to say how pleased I am about the way you've brought on the children. They're taking to it like ducks to water. And as for Sandra, I admit you've been proved right in this case.'

In spite of her resolutions, Briony felt herself glow a little. There was one thing about Blane, she admitted grudgingly—he might be sparing in his praise but, as Johnny had pointed out, he was always fair. All the same, would she ever learn to comprehend him? she wondered.

'But that's not what I want to speak to you about,' he went on.

She sat bolt upright, listening warily.

'Senga has been telling me that Miss Anderson is quite taken with the idea of the treasure hunt and I want to iron out the details with you. If we put our heads together we can settle most of the problems here and now. It's altogether a better suggestion than trekking. Kids are avaricious little creatures, and the prospect of a prize at the end of the hunt will appeal to them. Well, what do you say?'

'I'd like to help, of course,' she said slowly. 'But, after all, this wasn't my idea!'

'You feel I should have asked Senga to help? I would too, but she's too busy at the moment. Anyway, I think you'd make a good job of this, although I'd better warn you that there's going to be a lot of downright hard work involved. The children hunt in pairs. Clues are made up, which lead them forward from place to place, until they discover the treasure. Speed in deciphering the clues is, of course, important, and the prizes go to a great extent to the most quickwitted. And also to the best riders, of course! As the children are so young, the clues had better be hidden in easily recognisable places. At first I thought of having them hunt along Deeside, but perhaps it would be better to have it on ground they're familiar with. All the same, during the hunt they'll have to be watched, because some of them are downright silly, and can get up to dangerous things when they get exited and carried away. I'm leaving the clues in your hands. They ought to be rhyming, which is a darned nuisance for the adults involved, but fun for the kids. Still, I imagine it will be your cup of tea. Devising the clues should suit you down to the ground, for you can be quick enough with your tongue when you want to,' he added dryly. 'Well, do you feel you could cope? Of course you could,' he put in before she could reply. 'There's nothing you don't seem to know about kids. And that's one reason why I've asked you.'

Briony swallowed. She hadn't quite digested what was

expected of her. 'I think I can,' she muttered.

'Of course you can!' he told her. 'I'll take a look around tomorrow and decide on the best spots to plant the clues. The prizes might be a cut above the average, perhaps. Sweets are the usual thing, but I thought of giving a couple of little trinkets—little silver bangles, perhaps, or some such thing that little girls would like. And another thing, we must have Mrs McPhee lay on a slap-up tea to round off the affair. I want to make sure this is a success. I'm running this place for profit and nothing must go wrong. An accident to one of the kids, for example, would be very bad publicity for me.'

How typical of him to discuss the matter so bluntly, Briony was thinking.

'You'll have to put on your thinking cap and get to work on those clues. Nothing too obscure! At the same time nothing too obvious, or it will be no fun for the children.'

Briony smiled wryly. 'You want it every way, don't you?'

He nodded and, hands in pockets, strode up and down the room. 'Yes, I expect I do. But then I aim for the best—the best riding school in this part of the country, and the best crew I can lay hands on to run it! I want to turn out the best riders. And, when the time comes——' he hesitated, and turning, stared frowningly through the window, 'well, the best wife that a man can have.'

For a moment there was silence, but it was an electric silence. Awareness encompassed them like a wizard's spell. Briony drew a deep breath. 'The Dutch barn in the ten-acre would be a good place to plant the first clue, wouldn't it?' she heard herself ask, her voice unnaturally high.

Blane nodded. 'Yes, and for a second clue——' He beckoned her towards him and she joined him at the window. 'Do you see down there?' He pointed. 'That enormous granite boulder? That would be another obvious place—easily recognisable.'

She was close to him now, scarcely aware of what he was saying, her emotions in turmoil. Something had happened during this interview which had cast her into complete confusion. How could it be possible that, although she intensely disliked this man, she now wished to prolong the moment as long as possible, putting off the time when, in his brusque way, she would be dismissed?

It was just then that Mrs McPhee announced Senga.

For a moment the games mistress stared at them in blank astonishment, then her glance came to rest on the map by the window. 'You two look as if you're planning a battle.'

'Let's hope it doesn't turn into one,' Blane said dryly. 'We're having a confab about the treasure hunt. At first I thought of planting clues along Deeside—hence the map. But some of the kids are a bit wild and woolly, so we'd better keep them nearer home. It will be easier to locate them if anything goes wrong. Briony is getting to work on the clues right away.'

'Really?' Senga said tightly, her cheekbones bright with anger. 'I hadn't realised Briony knew anything about organising a hunt! According to her, the egg-and-spoon race was about her form when she was a kid.'

'Perhaps,' Blane said coolly. 'But she's a bit older now and seems to have a wonderful understanding of children, and also seems to be an expert at smoothing out tantrums. It's pretty important in this game, I think you'll realise.'

'All the same,' Senga put in quickly, 'I've experience of these hunts, and I must say I think my advice would have been more useful to you than Briony's.'

'Look, Senga,' he told her, 'with children, you must admit, you're not exactly sympatica. I mean, you don't even *want* to be the motherly type, do you?'

'I should hope not!' Senga retorted. 'You know perfectly well that's not what I mean! If Briony wants to soothe the children that's her business. But *I* could have done the planning!'

'But I don't *want* you to do the planning. I want you to spend every spare moment practising for the competition. We can't have you disgracing the Lennox Riding School.'

'That's only an excuse,' flashed Senga. 'I have plenty of free time, and I know how things should be done. It's early days yet! After all, we only thought of this recently, and——'

Briony was aware that impatience was building up in her employer.

'I want this idea carried out quickly,' he told Senga, his brow darkening, 'and Briony's capable of taking on the whole caboodle herself!'

'I see! So you're going to rush this thing through with Briony's help?'

'I don't believe in letting projects hang in the air for weeks at a time,' he told her, 'and I'm quite sure your precious Miss Anderson will be satisfied. We intend to present prizes of a high quality, don't we, Briony?'

Briony glanced away uncomfortably, as Senga turned towards her, her eyes narrowing suspiciously.

'So you already have this whole thing sewn up? Well, don't let me delay you. I can see you're both busy.' And, swinging around, Senga crashed the door behind her furiously.

A few mornings later Briony sat in the tack room, a mug of tea at her elbow, pencil and paper before her, as she struggled to compose the first clue.

She took a sip of the strong tea and was biting into the iced bun which accompanied it when a shadow fell across the doorway and Blane appeared.

With a little twinge of alarm Briony glanced up. He

would be annoyed to see her spinning out the morning break in this fashion, and she could hardly tell him that she was lurking in the tack room because she did not want to be in the stable-yard when Senga put in her appearance. Senga, she felt, would hardly be in an amiable mood.

'I'm—I'm working on the clues,' she said quickly, as he took a girth from one of the hooks against the wall.

'And how are you getting along?'

With relief, she knew from the tone of his voice that he was not angry. 'I'm having difficulties with the very first clue—the one that leads to the Dutch barn,' she told him. 'I don't seem to be able to find anything to rhyme with Holland.'

'Let me see—Holland.' He paused for a moment, then said, 'You're quite right—there doesn't seem to be anything to rhyme with it. You'll have to use the word Dutch, although it rather gives the game away, doesn't it?'

'It might be as well if the first clue were rather simple,' she told him. 'It would get things going. And after all, they're only children.' She scribbled for a moment and then said, 'This is not very good, I know, but perhaps it would do.

> *"Follow your pony's nose*
> *And he will lead you to something Dutch.*
> *Let him nibble a bit,*
> *But not too much."*

The last line is to give the hint that the next clue is hidden under the hay.'

'Yes, that should get things going,' he agreed. 'And later clues might be a bit more difficult. By the way, how is it that you get along so well with children? Do you come of a big family? Plenty of brothers and sisters, or perhaps nieces and nephews if you're the youngest of your family?'

'No, not a big family,' she replied. 'And it was by accident I found I had a way with children. There's a club near us that runs outings and other events for deprived children and I used to go along and lend a hand. Right away, I found that I was getting along with them, although some of them were difficult enough—from broken homes, and that sort of thing.'

'A natural gift, it seems,' he said thoughtfully. And as he went out, he added, 'Perhaps the reason is that there's still a lot of the child in yourself.'

So that was how he regarded her, Briony was thinking with annoyance. In his own mind he was contrasting her with the sophisticated Senga.

Almost immediately the station-wagon from Laureston School arrived. With a swift, lithe movement Senga slipped from behind the wheel, leaving the children milling about in the stable-yard, and went to join Blane, who was leading out Golden Sovereign. They moved away in the direction of the paddock in which Senga usually practised jumping.

The coast clear, Briony emerged from the tack room and as she did so became aware that the children were unusually excited. Soon the reason was clear—Senga had already announced the forthcoming treasure hunt. This meant that for Briony the business of getting her pupils mounted was even more difficult than usual, because each child now demanded to be given what she felt was the swiftest pony. Briony had to exercise considerable tact before she could get them on their way to the paddock in which the lesson was to take place.

But there was still Sandra to be dealt with.

As she followed them, Briony discovered with alarm that the child was once more in her old place, perched on the top rail of the paddock. Dismay made her speak more sharply than she intended. 'Where's Teddy? Have you grown tired of him already?'

Sandra slid off the rail and came towards her. 'I was

waiting to speak to you,' she said reproachfully. 'I want to ride a pony today, but it's not because I don't love Teddy any more. It's because none of the others will ride with me if I go to the treasure hunt on him. He's too slow, you see. I must learn to ride like the wind, so that we can get there first and win the prizes.'

Briony looked at the eager young face turned up to hers, and sighed. Trust Sandra to present her with a problem like this just when she was at her busiest! But she could not bring herself to refuse. 'Very well,' she said. 'You may have a pony, if you'll give me your word that this time you'll learn to ride properly. But you can't begin today. You'd better ask Miss MacNeil to bring you with her when she comes for her own lesson tomorrow. Now go and fetch Teddy and you can ride about on him for a while.'

The date for the jumping competition was drawing close and Senga was taking lessons nearly every day. Her eagerness to become as adept as possible was matched by Blane's interest; he always made time to instruct her himself.

Sandra, it was soon clear, had carried out Briony's instructions and had asked permission to have special lessons, because on the next occasion when Senga arrived, Sandra was with her.

Ignoring Briony, Senga went immediately to join Blane, who had already led the palomino to the jumping paddock, while Briony mounted her pupil on a docile pony and working with the lungeing rein began to give her exercises calculated to develop poise and balance in the saddle.

And now Briony was amazed at the difference she found in this once difficult pupil. Sandra, she discovered, was all eagerness and attention.

Instructing her to take her feet out of the stirrups, Briony taught her to swing her arms down and touch her toes, to throw her arms up and swing them in a circle backwards, to swing around from the waist, first to the right and then to the left, resting between each exercise and then repeating it slowly.

This was not easy for Sandra, who had been accustomed to clinging to the reins and to resting her feet heavily on the stirrups, but she persisted doggedly until Briony called a halt to the lesson.

From that time forward Briony found that she had almost more to do than she could fit into the working hours of the day. Gradually the grooming and general care of the ponies ridden by the children had fallen to her lot, especially the Shetlands, and in these Briony took a special interest. She soon found too that Blane had been speaking the truth when he had warned her that there was a great deal of work involved in the organising of the treasure hunt. And, what with special lessons to be given to Sandra, it was not surprising that at the end of the day she was glad to hurry back to the cottage and tuck into the meal which Hettie had prepared for her.

All in all Briony was delighted when the day of the show-jumping competition arrived to make a break in the usual routine. Briony did not have to give lessons because her pupils had all set off in a specially hired mini-bus to watch their games mistress compete. Blane of course attended, while Johnny drove Golden Sovereign in a motorised horse-box.

As soon as all was quiet in the stable-yard Briony took advantage of the lull to run an eagle eye over the tack under her care, with a sharp lookout for weak patches or loose stitches. This done, there were plenty more tasks to be attended to, and the day flew.

She was still hard at it when that evening Johnny drove the horse-box into the yard. He stepped out, a pleased grin on his face. 'Guess how Senga did in the competition?' he asked.

'I can see from the expression on your face that she did well,' Briony told him.

'She did! Took first place. And you should have seen the competition she was up against! There were some very experienced riders there.'

'I'm glad she did well,' Briony told him sincerely.

'You're not half as pleased as the boss is!' Johnny returned. 'He's tickled pink. And why shouldn't he be? It's a great advert for the Lennox Riding School. He's rewarding Senga with a champagne dinner tonight—just the two of them.'

'Well, Senga has earned it,' Briony told him, busily taking hold of the wheelbarrow she had been pushing, as she saw Johnny glance at her slyly out of the corner of his eye. 'I'm delighted for her.'

'Are you?' he teased. 'Something tells me that at this very moment you're wishing it was you who was going out this evening for dinner with the boss.'

'Now you're being silly, Johnny,' she told him loftily.

'Am I? Do you think I don't notice that "certain something" in the air when you're together?'

'Really, Johnny!' Briony tried to sound condescending. 'You're too young to know what you're talking about. If there's anything "in the air", as you call it, it's probably the dreadful smell of the bean mash you keep boiling on the stove.'

But Johnny wasn't to be sidetracked. An impudent grin split his boyish face as he turned away bawling 'Love in Bloom' at the top of his voice and with marked emphasis.

CHAPTER SEVEN

As Briony turned away she caught sight of a small figure cycling along the drive in a rather wobbly fashion. 'Sandra!' she cried, 'what are you doing here?'

'I've come for my lesson,' Sandra replied rather breathlessly, as she propped the bicycle against the wall of one of the loose-boxes. 'Remember, you promised to show me how to trot properly.'

'Yes, so I did!' Briony agreed. 'But I thought you'd be at the show-jumping today.'

'Oh, I went all right,' Sandra assured her. 'And Miss MacNeil was simply wonderful. She looked just beautiful flying over the jumps on Golden Sovereign and——'

Briony sighed. Sandra's arrival had put paid to her hope of catching up with her chores before Blane's return. 'Very well, now that you're here, you may as well have your lesson,' she broke in.

The lesson that afternoon was difficult—as usual— and Briony had to remind herself that, as Sandra made heavy weather even out of the simplest movements in riding, it was not surprising that she found the trot a stumbling block. Sandra was inclined to drop heavily into the saddle after the rise and to push herself up from the stirrups. Patiently Briony repeated her instructions over and over again, giving her plenty of practice, but, as so often happened with untalented riders, Sandra was rather worse at the end of the lesson than she had been at the beginning.

As Briony led the pony back towards the stable-yard, Sandra walked by her side, looking very solemn. Unexpectedly she asked, 'Do you like Miss MacNeil?'

'Yes, of course,' Briony replied, wondering where this question was leading.

'I didn't like her myself—not at first,' Sandra confessed. 'You see, she was always saying I was a terrible show-off and a notice-box, and that wasn't a nice thing to say, you know.'

'Well you must admit, Sandra,' Briony told her, 'you *were* a bit of a notice-box.'

Sandra thought this over for a moment or two. 'I suppose you're right,' she agreed reluctantly. 'But I'm better than I was, aren't I?'

'Yes, indeed you are,' Briony told her warmly. 'You're quite different now.'

'I'm glad of that,' Sandra said solemnly, 'because I want Miss MacNeil to like me. When I saw her jumping on Golden Sovereign today I felt so glad and proud. I only wish I were prettier, and then she might let me be one of her bridesmaids, and——'

'Bridesmaids?' queried Briony. 'Is she getting married?'

'But of course.' Sandra lowered her voice confidentially. 'Everyone says they're going to announce their engagement at any moment.'

'And who is she getting engaged to?' asked Briony, although she guessed what the answer would be.

Sandra looked surprised. 'To Blane Lennox, of course! She's *madly* in love with him. Everyone knows that! Maybe he'll give her the ring this very evening. Wouldn't it be lovely and romantic?' she added dreamily. 'Perhaps he'll gently slip it on to her finger over a candlelit table with music softly playing in the background.' She sighed ecstatically.

So Sandra had caught wind of the celebration dinner!

'They're going out together because she did so well at the competition and made him so proud of her,' Sandra told her rapturously. 'He's madly in love with her—just as she is with him. Of course she's not beautiful—not

strictly beautiful, that is, but she's so elegant and soignée—and that's more important, I think. Don't you?'

But by this time they had reached the stable-yard.
'Now how about getting you back to the school,
Sandra,' Briony broke in briskly. 'I'd better drive you
back. You've had just about enough exercise for one
day.'

But Sandra protested vehemently. 'Oh no, I'm going
to cycle back again. Daddy got it for me specially. It
folds up, you see, and you can fit it into the trunk of a
car, it's so very small. But at the same time, it goes like
the wind.'

'Do be sensible!' Briony urged. 'It's quite a long way
and the road through the moors is so very lonely.'

'But I'm not tired, not really,' Sandra said as she took
her cycle from the stable wall. 'And I shan't be the
smallest bit lonely. You can see the school when you're
a long way off, so you feel you're nearly there, even
when you've still got a distance to go. And don't worry,
I shan't get lost, because I know that part of the country
like the back of my hand. You see, we often go out on
paperchases and I can find my way across the moors
like a bloodhound.'

Afterwards Briony was to blame herself for not insisting on driving the child home, but at that moment
Sandra looked so eager and so proud of her new toy
that she yielded.

'I suppose you'll be all right,' she said reluctantly. 'Just keep on the road and you'll get there in the
end.'

Sandra took off her riding hat and, putting it in the
neat white box behind her saddle, mounted her cycle
and rode off.

She had hardly gone when Blane's car drove into the
yard. 'Was that Sandra I saw going past on a very diminutive cycle?' he asked, as he got out.

'Yes, it's a new toy of hers,' Briony smiled. 'She's

really been very good. She cycled all the way from the school for her lesson. She's very keen.'

'And is she going to cycle back? Isn't she rather young for so much exercise in one day?'

'I did offer to drive her back,' Briony said quickly. 'But she insisted and——'

'And you gave way!'

'Yes,' she admitted. 'Perhaps I shouldn't have—but she seemed so pleased, and there's so little Sandra is really good at, and——'

'Oh well, she'll probably arrive in one piece, although it may take her a while. After all, it's a straight road. She can't lose her way. And now tell me how you've got on since I saw you last.'

'I had a look through the tack for the Shetlands,' Briony told him. 'There are a few pieces which are pretty badly worn, and——'

But it was clear he was hardly listening. 'I suppose you have heard the news?' he asked. 'Senga came first. Johnny probably told you.'

'Yes, it must have been wonderful,' she said enthusiastically.

'She's not experienced in competition conditions, and perhaps it was a bit of a fluke, but she has plenty of courage and that carried her through. To take first place against the riders she had to compete with was a real triumph. Oh yes, all in all I think we can say we've had quite a successful day.'

He took a few restless steps about the stable-yard. 'But now it's over and we must push on to the next thing—and that's the treasure hunt. We must make a success of that too. By the way, we haven't fixed on a spot in which the prizes could be hidden. Has anything struck you?'

'What about the hollow in the oak tree by the burn?' Briony suggested. He looked at her enquiringly, and she went on, 'You may not have noticed it, but there's a hollow in the bark on the far side of the trunk. There's a nook inside in which one can hide things—I used to do it myself when I was a child.'

'Sounds just what we need!' he agreed. 'But perhaps you'd better show it to me. Could you possibly come back after tea and we'll take a look at it?'

When Briony entered the cottage she found Hettie dressed to go out. 'You're a bit late this evening,' she commented, as she pulled on her gloves, 'but there's a casserole in the oven and I've baked an apple tart. It's cooling on the table by the window and there's a jug of cream to go with it.'

When Hettie had gone off to the dressmaking lessons which were held in the Church Hall Briony went through the living-room and into the bathroom at the back of the cottage. It was too tiny to house a full-length bath, but had an excellent shower. Briony wore no shower cap, but allowed the water to pour over her hair, then towelled it dry and rapidly set it into a smooth cap-like style with her fingertips. She put on a fresh white blouse and pullover and clean jeans, then went into the kitchen to take the casserole out of the oven.

But the care Hettie had put into her cooking was wasted on Briony. As she ate she was in a rebellious mood. Thanks to Senga, this had been a successful day for Blane. But already in his restless mind the triumph was moving into the past. Let's push on to the next thing! That was his attitude. It was just a chance that the next thing happened to be the treasure hunt. Hurry home, have your tea quickly and then hurry back so that we can get on with the organising of the hunt— that was what he wanted. And suddenly she felt she could not endure another moment of it.

She glanced down at her clothes. Tidy and clean, yes—but the same rig in which he always saw her! What if she were to look different for a change? If she were to put on something attractive—something utterly feminine, perhaps Blane would think of her as a human being for once. She was tired of being accepted as part of the background at Birchfields; always there, almost invisible in her practical gear.

She put down her knife and fork and ran upstairs. In her own room she slipped off her workaday clothes and put on a pretty dress in a synthetic material. It was nothing very special, just a light summer dress, but the pattern of bright discs of emerald green and blue and yellow made it attractive. With it went fine hose and smart sandals. Quickly she ran a comb through her hair and fluffed up the tips with her fingers. A touch of lipstick completed a very light swift make-up.

She glanced at her watch. She had been as quick as possible, but still she knew, being well aware of how Blane hated to be kept waiting, that she would have to hurry.

When she arrived she found him standing in the doorway of the house. This made her last few steps rather a selfconscious matter, and as she approached she was expecting with a rather prickly tenseness some comment on her appearance.

But all he said was, 'You brought no coat, I see. The evening has turned chilly.'

Briony could have told him she hadn't noticed any chill in the air because she had been hurrying, but decided to keep this to herself.

He opened the door of a cupboard in the hall, pulled out a duffle coat and throwing it about her shoulders, cape-fashion, fastened the top peg under her chin. 'There! A bit too big perhaps, but at least it will keep you from getting your death of cold.'

As he moved away from the house she found herself hurrying to keep up with him, the long sleeves of the duffle coat dangling by her sides. What a complex person Blane Lennox was, she was thinking. He could be so harsh and demanding at times, asking of people

Love Beyond Reason

KAREN VAN DER ZEE

Love Beyond Reason

Karen van der Zee

CHAPTER ONE

It had been a terrible mistake; Amy realised it as soon
as she saw Vic's face—hard and cold with anger. A
shiver ran down her back and her legs felt wobbly. He
didn't look at all like she remembered him. Was this
really Vic, this stranger with the three-day growth of
beard, the deep tan, the dusty old jeans? There was a
squareness about the dark head, a hard muscularity
about his body that she didn't recognise. Standing there
in the middle of all those people wearing strange
clothes—saris and turbans and veils—everything
seemed unreal to her. Was this a nightmare? A halluci-
nation? An optical illusion? She closed her eyes briefly,
wanting to shut out the alien world around her, the
strangeness of that big man in front of her. When she
looked again he was still standing there, silent like a
rock, with his feet slightly apart and his hands in his
pockets, his eyes still angry. Amy felt sick and dizzy with
everything around her swirling in mad circles.

No wonder! She hadn't seen a bed for over thirty
hours and she was exhausted. The last few nights she
had hardly slept at all, kept awake by excitement and
the longing to see him again. Taking a deep breath, she
anchored her feet to the floor to steady herself and
bent down to pick up her suitcases. Her hair fell forward, blocking everything from view, and for a fleeting
moment she wished she could hide for ever behind the
dark curtain of hair. She straightened, tossing it back
behind her shoulders with a swift movement of her
head, and then Vic took a step forward, grabbed her by
the arm, quite ungently, and swung her closer. The
suitcases dropped from her fingers and she almost lost
her balance.

Read the rest of "Love Beyond Reason" FREE—plus get 3 more FREE BOOKS from Harlequin!

Find out what happens next. Let us send you the rest of "Love Beyond Reason" plus three more thrilling romance novels, as your FREE introduction to the Harlequin home subscription plan. Mail the coupon today!

**EXTRA BONUS
MAIL YOUR ORDER
TODAY AND GET A
FREE TOTE BAG
FROM HARLEQUIN.**

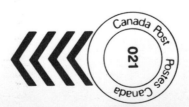

Canada Post
Postes
Canada
021

almost more than they could give, then unexpectedly could show a rough consideration that made one forget his past offences.

He turned along by the burn into which Sandra had fallen during that very first lesson that Briony had ever given at Birchfields, and as they came level with a solitary oak-tree on the opposite bank, he paused. 'Is this the tree? A hollow on the far side, I think you said. Better stay here while I have a look. If you paddle across the burn in those shoes they'll never be the same again!'

He leaped across the narrow stream, thrust aside some shrubs that grew behind the tree and began to feel along the bark. 'Yes, here it is. And this should be ideal. The bushes conceal the hole, even after the tree is discovered, and that's all to the good.'

As he returned to her side of the stream he said, 'We could have a little of the wood carved out, because the hole inside is rather small. But, apart from that, it's the very thing we need. None of the children are aware of its existence, I suppose?'

'Not that I know of,' she replied. 'In fact it had completely slipped my own mind. It was just by chance that I thought of it.'

'You used to hide things in it when you were a child. What sort of things?'

'Oh, half-sucked soor plooms, and bits of chocolate and toffee bars. You see, when Uncle Roy gave me pocket-money I used to spend it right away in Annie Skinner's shop. But Hettie didn't like me to spoil my appetite by eating between meals, so I had to hide away the goodies.'

'You know, when you said you used to hide things in the hollow I pictured them as being something else,' commented Blane.

She looked at him enquiringly.

'I wondered if you had had a childish love affair with some little fellow in Abergour—someone you used to exchange love-letters with, using the hollow as a post-box! Someone you might have wanted to come back and see again.'

'What on earth do you mean?' Briony asked in surprise.

'I mean, just in case he still carried the torch for you.'

Briony laughed. 'Oh, nothing like that! I'm afraid sweets were my main preoccupation in those days.'

'So you didn't even have a crush on someone in a childish way? I see. So if you were to fall in love with someone here in Abergour it would be for the first time?'

For a moment Briony felt herself overcome by self-consciousness. She glanced away hastily in case unintentionally she might reveal how his words had struck home.

But when she didn't answer he quickly changed the subject.

And just as well, she thought, because she might inadvertently have given away that she had indeed fallen in love—but with him.

'I don't think you've seen the flat,' he was saying.

'Flat?' she asked in surprise.

'Did you not know that part of the agreement when your godmother sold the house was that she should retain the upper storey?'

Briony looked at him in bewilderment. 'No. She never mentioned it.'

Blane gave a wry smile. 'No, I suppose not! As I'm not her favourite person she's hardly likely to include that little detail in the history of my life! But come along, and I'll show it to you. It was all done up before she took over. As the house was sold with its contents I agreed that she should pick out her favourite pieces and furnish her flat with them.'

As they walked towards the side of the house he went

on, 'It has two bedrooms and all the usual appointments, as they say in the advertisements.'

Feeling bewildered by this unexpected piece of news, Briony went with him to a spot where outside stairs guarded by silver-painted iron railings led upwards to a small balcony. And now she realised that while she had often noticed these stairs she had vaguely accepted them as part of the alterations he had made to the house.

Now, as they ascended the stairs to the balcony surrounded by lace-like ironwork, she realised that this reminded her of pictures she had often seen of houses in New Orleans.

When Blane had opened the door that led off the balcony she found herself in a long white passageway, and immediately she got an impression of light and cleanliness. From the long skylight which ran the length of the corridor light flooded down on to an amber carpet.

'Mrs McPhee sees this place is kept tidy and clean all the time just in case your godmother might some time wish to return,' he told her, as he opened one of the doors on the right of the corridor. 'This is the sitting-room.'

Briony gazed around in wonderment. The room wasn't very big, but it was beautifully furnished with wall-to-wall carpeting. The walls were silver-white and the furniture was a mixture of good modern and antique so that nothing seemed to clash.

As he showed her one room after another, Briony found her wonderment growing. How on earth could Hettie have turned her back on such an exquisite little jewel of a flat!

The kitchen too was perfect in every detail. It gleamed with pristine cleanliness and contained the most up-to-date equipment.

'This cost a pretty penny, I can tell you,' Blane told her, as Briony moved about the kitchen examining the micro-wave cooker, the electric mixer and other electric gadgets, all to hand upon spotless pale green work surfaces.

She shook her head in bewilderment when at last they returned to the balcony. 'I can't imagine why Hettie should have given up such a wonderful flat. The cottage, of course, is quaint, but—well, give me modern conveniences every time.'

'From what I gather your godmother is not very keen on her present quarters, is she?'

Briony shook her head. 'No, she grumbles a bit, I must admit. It all sounds so mysterious. Did she give any reason why she left?'

Why was it Hettie had abandoned this convenient flat and gone to Amulree Cottage? What was behind it all? Briony was asking herself uneasily.

'She gave no reason. Your guess is as good as mine,' Blane told her as they reached the ground once more. 'But I can assure you that as far as the flat is concerned there are no strings attached. It was part of the agreement. I had no intention of throwing your godmother on the scrapheap, just because I'd bought her home.'

'All the same, not many people would have gone to such trouble to see that everything was right for her,' Briony told him. 'After all, you owed her nothing. You'd bought a property that was going downhill anyway. Even when I was a child I realised that things at Birchfields were very neglected.'

'Well, that's the way things are! But I thought you might like to see it anyway, because I had the feeling you hadn't been told about it. And anyway, I don't want one more nail in my coffin,' he ended wryly.

As they reached the front of the house they paused and after a moment Briony said rather awkwardly, 'Thank you for showing me the flat. I must say I was worried about Hettie, but now—well, I feel so much better about everything.'

'As long as you're content that's all that matters,' Blane replied.

'Well, I'd better be getting back,' she said. 'Hettie will be wondering what's become of me. I'll let you have your coat.' As she spoke she was unfastening the toggle at her throat.

'Just a moment,' he said. 'It's growing dusk. I'm wondering if I ought to drive you home. I wouldn't have two thoughts about it, but as it happens I have an appointment this evening——' he looked at his watch.

'But it's still quite bright,' she protested, 'and somehow I never feel the smallest bit afraid here in Abergour.'

But as she was about to turn away, he detained her. 'By the way, do you think you'll have trouble thinking of a clue leading to the treasure?'

'It struck me that King Charles the Second hid in the hollow trunk of an oak tree when he was fleeing from his enemies,' Briony said, 'and I thought this might be used in the clue. It will make it more difficult, but after all that would be quite fair, because this will be the last clue.' Rather apologetically she went on, 'I don't know if anything like this would do, but here it is:

"*Look where King Charles hid when from his enemies he did flee.*
You may find an acorn, or the treasure you may see."

She wasn't too surprised to hear his burst of laughter. 'It's easy to see you're no lover of poetry!'

'Oh, but I am,' she protested. 'I know I can't *write* poetry, but I love to read it.'

'Is that so?' His voice held amusement. 'Come in a moment, and I'll try to rout out something helpful.'

When they went into the house he led her into what at one time had been the main sitting-room of Birchfields. But how different it looked now!

When he switched on the central lights Briony found

herself in a room that seemed much larger and more spacious, now that the clutter of Hettie's days had been swept away. In place of the worn, shabby furniture were broad modern armchairs covered in cream-coloured vinyl and brilliantly tinted rugs lay on the shining wood floor.

'Take a seat,' he ordered, as he crossed to one of the low bookcases against the walls. As he threw open the glass doors and plucked out a couple of volumes, Briony slowly laid his coat over the back of one of the armchairs and took a seat near the bright fire.

'Now here's the kind of thing I like,' Blane was saying. 'The old ballads, so simple that you'd think anyone could copy them, but full of good stories, like the one about the man from the North Country who stole away the bride on her wedding day. They believed in the success of first love in those days. If a new man came into the lady's life, the hero just rode in and abducted her.

> *"He's ta'en her by the milk-white hand*
> *And by the grass-green sleeve.*
> *He's mounted her behind himself,*
> *Of her kin he asked no leave." '*

His broad brown fingers rapidly turned the pages. 'They knew the price of love, these old poets. Here's the story of Willie who had to fight fifteen knights to win his fair lady.

> *"He has gone to his lady dear*
> *And given her kisses, many a one.*
> *Thou art my own, I have bought thee, dear love,*
> *And now we will walk the woods our lone."*

'A man doesn't have to fight fifteen knights to win his fair lady nowadays, but love can still cost a man as dearly; but here, you'd better look through this yourself.'

As he spoke he handed her the book.

She took it from him, opened it and pretended to be studying the pages, but she had a curious sensation of unreality, a breathless feeling as if she were being swept along too quickly in some great tide. She had never seen him in this mood before, never heard him talk like this! This was a new Blane Lennox—a person she had not even suspected existed.

The volume in her hands was beautifully bound in pale green with the title *Old Scottish Ballads* written on it in gold, and as she turned it in her hands it fell open at the flyleaf and she saw:

> *'Then win me, win me, if you will,*
> *For well I know you may.'*

and 'Senga' written in bold lettering with a great stroke of the pen underneath.

Briony, seated rigidly upright in her chair, was unconsciously turning over and over in her hands the volume of love ballads.

Blane was walking restlessly about the room, talking more to himself than to her. 'But then I don't suppose this means an awful lot to you. After all, you're very young and probably, apart from a few sentimental affairs, have no notion what a deep love is like.'

His bright penetrating eyes were fixed upon her and she gazed at him in speechless confusion. What if she were to reveal to him that she had known what it was to be madly, crazily, and completely in love?

For an instant she closed her eyes as she remembered Jeremy—his quick, utterly charming smile that could make the day brighten up for her. And how an angry word had cast her into the depths of misery!

What if she were to reveal to Blane that she had known heartbreak? Would it make a bond between them when he realised that instead of being the naïve and inexperienced girl he imagined her to be she had experienced all the bitterness of being rejected by Jeremy

Warne? But then, she reminded herself cautiously, Blane Lennox was a man of quick temper and unpredictable emotions. Was it not more likely he would feel nothing but contempt for her? No, she daren't risk confiding in him, no matter how much she longed to spill out her troubles.

But how clearly this had brought Jeremy before her mind, reminding her of a past she had tried to thrust behind her.

And yet she knew she did not want to bring this episode to a close.

In a very short time Blane would very likely bring this little chat to a short and brisk termination. After all, he would be having dinner with Senga in Aberdeen this evening and he would have to change and drive to Laureston to collect her. What attraction could she possibly hold for him that Senga wouldn't have a hundredfold? She could visualise the other girl dressed for the evening, looking almost beautiful in red silk, perhaps. Her dress floating about her tall slim figure, her hair drawn smoothly back to emphasise those high cheekbones, her wide mouth heavily lipsticked, she would be more elegant, more interesting than any other woman in the room.

And no doubt this would be the very night when Blane would propose! Surely this had been in his mind when he had reached for that volume of ballads? So that explained the strange uncharacteristic mood that seemed to hold him. He had really been speaking his thoughts aloud to her, probably no more aware of her presence than of the chair she was sitting on. And the thought struck her like a blow. She stood up. 'I'd—I'd better be getting home.' The words came from stiff lips.

She held out the book, but he said quickly, 'Keep it for a while. Take care of it. It was given to me by a friend and I wouldn't like to lose it.'

'I'll—I'll take good care of it and let you have it back

in a few days,' she heard her own voice say as though coming from a distance. All she wanted now was to be out in the dusk of the evening, to collect her thoughts to introduce some calm into the whirlwind that seemed to envelop her.

But as she spoke they could hear the phone ringing in the office across the hall.

When Blane went out, Briony left the sitting-room and began to move across the hall. But as she was about to leave the house, the door of the office was thrown open. 'That call was from Senga,' Blane told her. 'It seems Sandra hasn't arrived at Laureston yet.'

'What? But she left ages ago!' Briony exclaimed.

'I know. I saw her leave just as I returned,' he said. 'What on earth can have become of her? Well, one thing is clear—she'll have to be found. Senga is making up a search party of the older girls right away. And oh, by the way, she asked about you. I told her you were here and she wants to speak to you for a moment.'

CHAPTER EIGHT

IT was with reluctance that Briony entered the office and picked up the receiver. What would Senga have to say to her? Nothing pleasant, she felt sure! And she was right!

'I just wanted to ask you if you don't feel that you should have driven Sandra back to the school,' Senga's voice enquired. 'Blane tells me he saw her go off on that damned diminutive cycle of hers.'

'But I *did* offer to drive her back,' Briony said quickly. 'I thought she looked tired, you see, but she insisted, and——'

'She insisted!' Senga's voice broke in cuttingly. 'Sandra insisted—and you gave way to her! And yet Blane tells me you're a wonder with children. I must say that's not *my* idea of how children should be handled! Sometimes they have to be taken firmly for their own good. Anyway, you're out of it now. Blane's coming over right away and bringing Johnny and Andy with him to help in the search. You can go home and rest. You've done a good day's work—and managed to spoil my evening—but that will hardly cost you your night's sleep, I expect!'

And the receiver was abruptly replaced at Senga's end.

Briony found Blane waiting for her in the hall. He was wearing a windcheater and had put on rubber boots and was carrying a storm lamp. He flashed it on for a second and Briony saw that it had a powerful beam.

'This is my fault,' Briony said miserably. 'I should have insisted on driving Sandra back.'

'There's no use crying over spilt milk,' he replied.

'Come, get into the car and I'll drop you off at the cottage on my way to the school. Mrs McPhee has gone to rout out the two boys, and we'll pick them up on our way.'

'But I must have a part in the search,' Briony protested. 'After all——'

'After all, it was all your fault!' he broke in. 'Really, Briony, who on earth could tell what a child like Sandra will get up to? Any other child could have cycled home safely considering it's a perfectly plain, flat road with the school visible for miles—but not Sandra. She has a genius for being different. But this I do notice—that while at times you can be rather severe with the other children, you seem to feel that Sandra must never be corrected.'

'It's—it's just that she's rather a lame duck,' Briony defended herself, feeling rather foolish. 'She's easily discouraged, and one likes to encourage any little show of initiative.'

'Well, this is one show of initiative that's going to cost us dear. It just so happens that I had rather an important appointment this evening, but between you, you and Sandra have managed to put paid to it.'

'All the more reason why I should have a part in the search,' Briony said stubbornly.

'All right. I'll drop you off at the cottage for a moment and you can let your godmother know where you'll be. But I warn you, don't keep me waiting, or I'll go off without you.'

They found Johnny and Andy waiting by the gate. They piled into the back of the car and after a moment or two Johnny said on bated breath, 'How did she manage to get lost? The road's perfectly clear.' He turned to Briony. 'There's no chance she's run off, is there?'

'What?' Briony gasped. The idea had not occurred to her.

But to her surprise Blane said, 'The same thought crossed my mind, and that's why I'm taking you with us, Briony. You have more influence over the child than anyone else. If Sandra is up to mischief you might be able to coax her to behave.'

Give a dog a bad name, Briony was thinking indignantly. But she did not dare to defend Sandra openly. When she reflected that this should have been the evening when Blane became engaged to Senga, she was only surprised that he was not in a rage, instead of showing a sort of weary contemptuous resignation to the situation.

They drew up at the cottage. Briony was out of the car and racing along the path in a moment.

'Now just where have you been?' Hettie greeted her as soon as she put in an appearance. 'Don't tell me you've been all this time showing that Lennox man the hole in the oak tree?'

'Don't delay me, Hettie,' Briony pleaded as she turned towards the stairs. 'Sandra is lost, and we must search for her immediately.'

To her relief this diverted the kindhearted Hettie. 'Is that the little girl you were telling me about—the one who rides a donkey?'

'The very same,' Briony agreed. 'And Hettie, do me a favour! Make up a flask of coffee—the instant kind will have to do. Oh, and Hettie, if you could find the electric torch I could take it with me.'

She ran on upstairs and changed into warm slacks and a sweater. She put on sturdy ankle-length boots and tucked the ends of her slacks into them. There was no time to comb her hair, so she snatched up a cap made of creamy Aran wool surmounted by a pom-pom and pulled it on. Then, taking a rainproof jacket with capacious pockets, she ran downstairs.

Hettie had risen to the occasion. She hurried out of the kitchen with a big flask of coffee. 'Here, here it is,' she said. 'A good thing I had the kettle boiling! And here's the torch. The battery is still going, but I don't know how much longer it will hold out.'

'Thanks, Hettie.' Briony slipped on the jacket, stuffed the flask into one of the pockets and snatched up the torch. 'You've been wonderful. But don't wait up for me. We don't know what's happened to her, or how long it will take to find her. There's no use in sitting up worrying. Try to get some sleep.'

'You may be sure I'll get plenty of sleep tonight!' Hettie told her ironically. 'What do you take me for, Briony? I'll be waiting up for you when you return, with hot soup. Now be off!'

Trust Hettie to turn up trumps, Briony was thinking as she gave her godmother a hug and rushed out to the car.

'This must be the world's record for a quick change,' Blane remarked as he started the engine. 'I must say I didn't hope to see you for another ten minutes.'

'What's more, I brought a flask of coffee,' she told him triumphantly as she took her place beside him once more. 'If Sandra hasn't been able to find shelter, she's sure to be chilled this evening.'

After that there was silence in the car as in tense concentration they watched the road as the powerful beam of the headlights illuminated it.

'It's a complete mystery,' Blane said after a while. 'Where can that child have disappeared to—that is if she's not hiding somewhere trying to scare us and make herself important.'

'I don't believe she is,' Briony told him quietly. 'Sandra is doing her very best these days. The last I heard from her was that she was looking forward to her next lesson.'

'What exactly did she say?' Blane asked. 'Did she give any hint as to what was going on in that strange little mind of hers?'

'Let me think.' Briony wrinkled her brow. 'I warned her to keep to the road and she said she would, and she said that she could see the school from quite a distance. Then she said that she wouldn't get lost in this part of the country, because Senga takes the girls out on paper-chases and they've learned to find their own way back to the school. But surely——'

While she had been speaking the eyes of everyone in the car were fixed on the terrain through which they were passing, a wide expanse of moor, boulder-strewn and overgrown with heather and clumps of bracken.

'But surely even Sandra wouldn't be mad enough to attempt a short cut,' Blane ended for her. 'If I were you I wouldn't count on it. I only hope Sandra knows her way through the moor as well as she thinks. Over there to the east,' he pointed to a rise of ground which could be detected as the headlights swept through a slight bend in the road, 'there's a deep hollow where some quarrying work was carried on for a short while. The quarry was closed down, but the spot still remains dangerous. There's what amounts to a short cliff face, and if she fell over that she certainly would be in trouble.'

'But surely she must have been here while it was still light,' Briony protested.

'That's true,' he agreed. 'We may as well cease trying to figure it out, because we won't know the explanation until we find her.'

He stopped the car on the gravel sweep before the school. And here everything was a scene of activity. Senga, assisted by a few of the other teachers, was organising the older girls into search groups.

The two boys were out of the back of the car in a trice and went to get their instructions. Blane went forward to speak to Senga and more slowly Briony got out of the car. As she did so she caught sight of the book of ballads lying on the seat of the car. She picked it up and put it into one of the pockets of her jacket.

As she stood beside the car she saw Senga turn her head for a moment, fix her with an angry stare, and then return her attention to Blane once more. In her heart Briony could not blame the girl for this deliberate cut. She knew that had she been in Senga's place she would have felt the same.

She heard Blane speak of the disused quarry, and heard Senga say that it had been searched and that Sandra was not there.

It was not long before Briony found herself one of a small party setting out on the search. They followed in single file a path which was invisible to her, but which apparently these girls, shining their torches before them, were able to make out. In spite of their guidance Briony found herself stumbling and wandering from the path, and once or twice when she struck her foot against an outcrop of rock, she would have fallen had not one of the girls grasped her by the arm and held her up. At length, feeling she was holding them back, she told the girls to go ahead and that she would keep up with them as well as she could.

It could hardly have been a more difficult night for the search, Briony was thinking as she edged along in the wake of the others. A chill wind was blowing which carried away the voices of the girls ahead, so that when they called out instructions to her she had great difficulty in making out what they were saying. Clouds scudded across the sky, occasionally revealing a rather pale and watery moon, but when these closed in again the going seemed even more difficult than before. Gradually she became a little separated from the girls in front who were edging forward confidently, flashing their torches from side to side.

Briony, following more slowly, tried to imitate them. She cast her torch in wide sweeps over the gorse and boulder-strewn wilderness, and as she did so she thought she detected a silvery gleam behind a clump of bracken.

Cautiously she made her way around a large granite boulder that was in her way, only to discover that the gleam she had seen was the reflection of the moon shining for an instant on Sandra's bicycle. And to her amazement she found the child lying curled up on the ground beside her bicycle fast asleep.

She had great difficulty awakening Sandra, but eventually she sat up looking very dazed. 'Oh, I knew you'd find me,' she said at last, and burst into tears and sobbed on Briony's shoulder.

Briony helped her to her feet and seated her upon the boulder. She put her jacket about the child's shoulders. She felt in the pocket and took out the flask. 'Here, try to take a little of this,' she urged as she unscrewed the cap and poured out some hot coffee. But Sandra's hands were icy and her teeth were chattering. Briony had to help her to steady the plastic cup and hold it up to her lips. Sandra was able to take a few sips and then seemed a little better.

'What happened to you? We've all been so worried,' Briony asked.

'I don't know what happened,' Sandra replied in a dazed fashion. 'Not really. I was cycling along the road, and I looked over my shoulder for an instant. Next moment the cycle struck a big stone and I was thrown over the handlebars and landed right on my head. The next thing I remember I was walking through the moors carrying the bicycle, but no matter how hard I tried I could get no nearer to the school.'

'Carrying your bicycle!' exclaimed Briony. 'But why did you do that? It could have been collected later.'

'I didn't think of that. I was afraid to lose it,' Sandra explained. 'Because it's very small, but it was very expensive and Daddy would be furious if I lost it.'

'I see,' said Briony.

'I walked and walked and then I felt very tired and I thought I'd lie down for just a little while. But I must have slept for a long time, because it's dark now.' And Sandra burst into tears once more.

Briony soothed her as well as she could, but as she spoke her mind was on the problem of getting her back to the school. In the few minutes since she had found Sandra, the searchers had moved on quite a distance. She could see their lights flashing across the ground, but when she called they could not hear her.

'I think the best thing we could do is to try to get back to the school ourselves,' she said at last. 'Lean on me, and we'll go along very slowly.'

But she quickly found out that this plan wasn't going to work. Sandra seemed incapable of taking any steady course. She spun around and staggered, and before they had taken more than a few steps had fallen to the ground.

As Briony helped her to her feet, she said anxiously, 'I'm afraid you're badly concussed. The best thing would be for you to stay here. Sit on this boulder. Very soon, when the searchers are coming back on their way towards the school, they'll see you. But they may be a little while, so I'd better try to get back to the school and get help for you right away.' As she spoke she took off her cap of Aran wool and placed it on the child's head, knowing that the pale colour would be clearly visible to the searchers. 'You'll stay here and not move, won't you? And you won't fall asleep whatever you do,' she urged, as she flashed on her torch. The beam was rather weaker, but she hoped it would enable her to get back to the school.

'I won't budge,' Sandra promised. 'But please, do you think you could leave the torch with me? The moon has come out again, and you'll be able to see your way. And if I had some light I wouldn't feel so frightened. And I can always flash it on if I hear them coming.'

Briony hesitated, wondering if she would be able to

manage without it, then seeing how distressed the child was she reluctantly agreed.

'You'll be as quick as you can, won't you, because I feel terrible,' quavered Sandra.

The school could be seen for miles around, especially on this evening when every window was illuminated. She could easily find her way, Briony told herself. With a reassuring wave of the hand she set off as quickly as she could.

But very soon clouds rolled up again and she found herself feeling her way in the darkness, edging forward carefully, and sometimes even kneeling down to feel the path with her hands.

Matters were not too bad as long as the school was in sight, but after a while she descended into a shallow hollow from which it was no longer visible. Quickly she found she was wandering around in circles, making no progress, and she decided that she had better climb to a higher point from which she could see the landmark of the school once more. It would be well worth while making a detour for the sake of having it in sight.

Off to the east was a point of higher ground, and as the moon came out again she ran forward, hoping to get to the top of the rise by its light. Here the ground was gravelly. Her foot slipped on the uneven moving surface and she found herself hurled forward and downwards. She suffered scratches, but came to no real harm, and to her surprise she found herself on a fairly even track which was partially overgrown with grasses and weeds but seemed to be leading towards the school. Here, walking was much easier than on the higher ground, and as she went forward she found she was making far more progress than she had previously done.

The track began to cut into the ground and to widen, and after a while she could feel the firmness of a good surface beneath the rubber soles of her boots. She seemed to be on a paved road which was curving in the direction of the school and she felt certain that she was doing the right thing in following it. This was perhaps a way that had led towards the back of Laureston House in the days when horses and carts were in use and which was now no longer necessary when everything was delivered by van or car.

But as the level of the road sank ever more deeply she found that it was becoming difficult to see her way and that she had to go forward cautiously.

Suddenly the moon shone out very brightly and Briony stood still in alarm. She discovered she was standing on a great block of stone and that a short distance ahead was a sharp fall—not very deep but enough to have caused a nasty accident and broken bones should she have gone any further.

And now she knew where she was! The track had led her into the disused quarry. She found herself in the middle of a shallow bowl with stone rising in ledges on all sides. And as she turned to look back she saw that the narrow road had passed close to the edge of a wide pool which glimmered a sinister silver-grey in the moonlight.

She would have to retrace her steps. But even as she realised this, the moon became clouded and she found herself standing in darkness. She would wait until she had light again before setting out on the return journey.

Unfortunately as the night progressed the patches of moonlight became less frequent, and eventually she had to admit to herself that the moon had set. There was nothing for it but to remain in the spot in which she found herself until the first light of morning.

She settled herself on a ledge of stone to wait. But as she ceased to be active she quickly discovered how keenly cold the night had become. She was wearing only slacks and a sweater, and as time passed she grew more and more chilled. In desperation she shouted as loudly as she could, but soon realised that the enclosed bowl-like shape of the shallow quarry was holding her voice and that it was not reaching up to the moor where the searchers were probably returning now to the school.

The main thing was not to panic, she told herself firmly. By this time they would have found Sandra, and Blane would be occupied in getting her back to the school. It would be some time before it was discovered that she, in her turn, was missing.

What a misfortune this was! Briony felt she would never be able to live down the frustrations and humiliations of this night. She had made one mistake after another. All she hoped now was that it would not be Blane who would find her. She shrank from meeting the regard of those vivid blue eyes. Far better that it should be Senga, no matter how cutting her remarks might be!

She leaned back against the wall of stone and closed her eyes, and in spite of the cruel cold which seemed to bite into her very bones, through sheer exhaustion she fell into a light doze.

Suddenly she was awake, aware that she had heard some strange sound.

She listened intently. Yes, there it was again—a curious tapping noise. As she stirred, it ceased immediately, but soon afterwards she heard it again. And as she watched, her eyes glued on the spot from which the sound seemed to come, she saw faintly perceptible in the darkness, the shape of antlers. So it was a deer she had heard! The tapping noise was the sound of its sharp hooves on the stony surface of the quarry. It would be sure to come nearer, she reflected, because she had often read of how inquisitive deer are. They will investigate anything that seems strange to them.

Then another thought struck her. Autumn is the only time of the year when a deer will attack a human being. Better perhaps not to let it come too close, lest, startled, it might strike at her with those great branching antlers.

She reached out her hand, and her fingers fell upon

some pebbles. She threw these in the direction of the animal and at the same time gave a loud shout, and to her relief she heard it bound away.

After that she shouted again and again, but eventually gave up and leaned back against the wall of rock once more. All her senses seemed numbed with cold and eventually she slept once more.

Next time she opened her eyes she found herself looking straight into Blane's face.

'So this is where you've been while I was searching for you!' was his remark. He lifted her down from her perch on the ledge of rock and set her on one of the great slabs of stone of which the quarry was composed. Then, taking off his jacket, he wrapped it around her. 'My turn now,' he remarked with a smile.

'What—what's that?' she asked, confused.

'I don't know if you remember,' he remarked, 'but you gave Sandra your jacket—and your cap too, come to think of it. That's how we found her. That pale-coloured cap of yours helped us to spot her.'

She tried to smile, but her face was stiff and to her mortification tears of exhaustion rolled down her cheeks.

'And now I'm going to leave you here for a while,' he told her. 'The girls have gone back to the school—they're quite done in after their night's exertions. Senga and the other teachers are pretty exhausted too. I sent Johnny and Andy back as soon as Sandra was discovered—I had no idea at that time that you were missing. I'll bring the car nearer, and then I'll be able to get you safely home, without having to disturb any of the others.'

'Go ahead,' she said quickly. 'I'm perfectly all right, now that I know you've found me.'

But once his footsteps had receded, every minute seemed an hour until his return.

He carried her to the car and laid her along the back

seat. Immediately, without a word, he took his place at the wheel and they set off.

After a while Briony said in a small voice, 'I seem to have given you a lot of trouble.'

She sensed rather than saw his face break into a grim smile. 'You're much too valuable an asset to the Lennox Riding School to be left to perish in a quarry.'

This reply was so unexpected that at once Briony's fighting spirit reasserted itself. 'Thanks,' she said huffily. 'I'm glad to know I'm of some value to you.'

He laughed outright. 'Were you really expecting a courtly compliment? Surely, Briony, you know me better than that, by this time!'

'All the same,' she answered snappishly, 'it wouldn't have done the Lennox Riding School much good if one of its wealthier pupils were lost. And if it hadn't been for me, she mightn't have been found at all.'

He considered this for a moment, then shook his head. 'You're wrong. She would have been found all right, but not as quickly.'

'I see.' She felt her ire rise at this nonchalant attitude. 'In other words I was wasting my time. I might as well have stayed at home and done nothing.' She turned her head around and looked out at the greyness beyond the window.

'Now you're talking nonsense!' he said, a slight irritation edging his voice. 'You did very well. There's no need to make a song and dance about it. We don't go in for heroics in this part of the country, you know. The people have a hard life and have learned to contend with it, without setting themselves up as heroes or heroines.'

Briony's temper came to boiling-point, and she began to twist at the handle of the door. 'Let me out! Let me out!' Her voice was muffled with anger. 'I'll walk the rest of the way.'

'You're a bit too late with the heroics!'

And feeling incredibly foolish, she saw that he was pulling up at the gate of Amulree.

He reached in and lifted her out of the back seat. Light blazed from the little cottage windows as he carried her along the narrow short path. Immediately the door was thrown open and in the burst of light, Briony saw that the bright Highland colouring had faded from Hettie's cheeks, and that her face looked grey and aged. 'What happened?' she cried as Briony was carried into the living-room.

'It's quite all right, Mrs Gillies,' Blane answered quietly. 'There are no bones broken, and apart from a few bruises and the fact that she's quite worn out, she's all right. But she's had to spend the night in the open, and I think you should send for the doctor right away. Now tell me, where does she sleep?'

Hettie pointed up the narrow stairs and he carried her up, and with great difficulty managed to negotiate the narrow strip of hall and to get Briony into her bedroom and lay her down on the soft mattress.

And now Briony made an attempt to thank him. 'You've been really wonderful to me. I don't know how to thank you. I'm so sorry about everything and——'

But he interrupted her stumbling efforts to make amends. 'Cheer up,' he said. 'The night is over at last, and it's not likely you'll have to go through anything like this again—at least, I hope, not for a long time.' With a wave of his hand he turned away and she heard his footsteps run down the stairs.

But the night was not over yet—at least not as far as she was concerned, for, to her horror, she could hear Hettie's voice quite clearly, raised in battle.

'And now, if you're quite finished with my godchild,' she was saying belligerently, 'you can get out of this house!'

Whatever Blane replied to this was inaudible to Briony, because his voice was low and measured. But once again she could hear Hettie's voice raised shrilly, 'I've made up my mind about one thing—she'll never work for you again. When she's recovered I'll make it my business to see that she keeps away from the Lennox Riding School!'

CHAPTER NINE

For the next few days Briony felt too ill to care much about anything.

Hettie proved a tower of strength. She did not spare herself, but laboured up the narrow stairs to Briony's room with hot-water bottles and bowls of nourishing soup.

But rapidly Briony recovered—she had youth and good health on her side, and soon she was receiving visitors. Annie Skinner arrived to survey the invalid and to assure her that she looked terrible. Hettie's friends from the dressmaking class called, with little presents and words of sympathy. A gift she valued especially was a bedjacket of quilted apricot-coloured fabric edged with white fur. She got a flood of get-well cards from her young pupils and two very comic ones from Johnny and Andy. But not a single word from Blane.

Sometimes in the afternoons, as she dozed off after one of Hettie's nourishing meals, she would wish wistfully that Blane might come to see her, but in her clearer moments she realised he would not come. He was not the kind of man who would tolerate Hettie's insulting words.

Then one day she had a very unexpected visitor.

She had fallen asleep after lunch, and woke up to the sound of Senga's voice in the sitting-room. She raised herself on her elbow, straining her ears to hear.

From what she gathered, Senga was in an affable mood. There was the clink of tea-cups and she could hear her say, 'Everything I've been told about your baking is quite true, Mrs Gillies. Your sultana scones are absolutely terrific!'

Briony heard Hettie's deep chuckle—always a sign that she was pleased. 'Oh, there's nothing to them, I can assure you. It just happens I have the knack.'

The next words Briony heard were, 'Then you're quite sure that Briony feels up to seeing me?'

'Och yes,' came Hettie's voice. 'She's quite on the mend, and I'm sure she'll be delighted to see a visitor. Go straight on upstairs. I shan't come with you, if you don't mind, because the stairs are very steep and I have to make so many trips up and down these days—and as you know, I'm not as young as I used to be.'

So Senga was coming up to see her! Briony slid out of bed and quickly ran a comb through her tousled hair. Then from the wardrobe she took her new bedjacket and slipped it on. Yes, the deep apricot shade lent a glow to her complexion and complemented the russet of her hair.

As she was getting into bed again she could hear Senga's footsteps lightly running up the stairs. But what could Senga have to say to her? Briony wondered, and had a sudden dread of this coming interview. Somehow it boded no good.

There was a short knock on the door and Senga's head appeared. 'May I come in?' she enquired sweetly. 'Am I disturbing you?'

'No, of course not,' Briony answered.

Senga settled herself on the end of the bed, crossed her legs and regarded the invalid, 'Well, your god-mother's right—you definitely look as if you're coming round. You'll be up and about in no time, I expect.'

Briony nodded, regarding the girl warily. There was something almost too self-possessed about her manner.

'I suppose you've gathered by this time that I'm really not the type to pay visits to sickbeds with jellies and sweet words, so I'll get straight to the point.'

Briony looked at her wide-eyed, wondering what was coming next.

For a moment Senga regarded the tips of her elegant sandals, then with a tight smile said abruptly, 'I suppose you remember the evening Sandra was lost. You should—after all, you have good reason to remember it. Well, that evening, when I rang to Blane to tell him Sandra was missing, I discovered you were at the house. Now why was that? After all, I think I've a right to know, considering how things are between Blane and myself.' She fixed Briony with a bleak eye.

'I—I——' To her annoyance Briony was aware that she sounded quite guilty. 'I was there because Blane asked me to come,' she said shortly. 'He wanted me to come back after tea.'

'Indeed!' Senga's eyebrows rose. 'And why on earth did he want that?'

'Because we hadn't decided on a hiding-place for the prizes—at the end of the treasure hunt, you see. And I knew of a hollow in the oak tree, and——'

But these details didn't interest Senga. She jumped to her feet, her face contorted with anger, and began to stride up and down Briony's small room.

'That treasure hunt!' she cried. 'I'm sick of the very sound of it! I wish I'd never thought of it! All day long I hear nothing else from the children at school, and now Blane is all wrapped up in it—madly keen to make a success of things. He's the kind of man who throws his whole heart into anything he tackles. That's his way. People don't exist for him when he's taken with one of his enthusiasms. But as far as I'm concerned, I've had more than enough of it!'

So that was what was troubling Senga, Briony thought. She was not getting enough attention. She wanted Blane's full concentration fixed on her, and would be content with nothing less.

As Briony gazed at her in amazement, Senga seemed to become aware of how irrational her behaviour appeared. With an effort she pulled herself together and sat down on a chair beside Briony's bed. 'But that's not really what I came to speak to you about,' she continued.

She opened the large black leather handbag she was carrying and took out something loosely wrapped in brown paper. She handed it to Briony and fixed her with an accusing glare.

Briony parted the brown paper and gasped as she saw the book of Scottish ballads which Blane had given her, but stained and discoloured almost beyond recognition. The once beautiful pale green cover was faded and muddied and some of the pages were torn.

'But—but—what happened to it? Where did you get it?' she gasped.

'So you recognise it!' Senga accused tightly.

'Why yes, of course,' Briony told her. 'It was in the pocket of the jacket I was wearing when I found Sandra.'

'The jacket which you so nobly wrapped around her,' Senga remarked. 'Quite the little angel of charity, weren't you?'

'I'm sorry,' Briony said weakly. 'I'd forgotten it was in the pocket. I mean, it's not the kind of thing you'd think about at a time like that.'

'It was found when they went to pick up her cycle. With her usual genius for mischief she'd let it fall in a patch of damp heather.'

'I wouldn't have had this happen for the world,' Briony said miserably.

'I'm quite sure you wouldn't,' Senga agreed sardonically. 'But as it *has* happened, perhaps you'd be good enough to let me know how it got into your hands in the first place. As you can see, it was a present from me to Blane.'

'We were talking about the clues, and—and—as I'm not very good at making up verses, he thought it might give me ideas, and——'

'He *gave* it to you?'

'But not to keep, of course,' Briony told her quickly. 'But he let me have it for a day or two—and he warned me to take good care of it,' she added placatingly.

'I see,' Senga replied. 'And what exactly do you intend to do about it? As you were responsible for its safe-keeping, I assume you have some ideas about its replacement.'

Briony looked at her in dismay. 'But how could I? I can see it's a beautiful old book. How could I ever get one like that again?'

'You're right,' Senga snapped, 'I don't think you could. I bought that in an auction of rare books. There's not the remotest chance you could lay your hands on one like it. Not unless you're prepared to scour the book-sellers—and pay through the nose as well!'

Briony felt her heart beat faster with dismay. 'Then what on earth can I do? I can't give it back to him like this! He'd be simply furious, especially as it's a gift from you!'

Senga could not restrain a slight smile of satisfaction. 'Yes, indeed! But that's exactly what I think you should do—face up to it and hand it back.'

Briony looked at her pleadingly. 'You couldn't give it back to him yourself? I mean, he wouldn't mind so much if it were you.'

'I wouldn't consider it for a moment,' Senga told her coldly. 'You got yourself into this mess and you can get yourself out of it. We're in love, you know. Very much in love! I think it might be as well for you, Briony, if you kept that strictly in mind. And I suggest you return that book as soon as possible. You're perfectly well now and you're not going to escape your responsibilities by skulking in bed. I'll leave you now to think of a few excuses—that's if you can find any convincing enough.'

And without waiting for Briony's reply she ran lightly down the stairs.

When she heard the door of the cottage shut behind Senga, Briony turned the book over in her hands. She was shocked anew by its look of dilapidation. This was a book that had been precious to Blane because it had been a present from the woman he loved. How was she going to face him? She flinched at the thought of what he would say to her when she returned it. But Senga had been right—it would have to be done! And she had no possible excuse for delay. She was fully recovered, and the sooner it was done the better.

On the following morning she got up very early, tiptoed into the kitchen and made herself a cup of tea. Hettie was a light sleeper and Briony dreaded the thought of awakening her and of having to face the angry scene which would undoubtedly take place. Hettie was determined she should not return to the Lennox Riding School, and Briony was equally determined to do all in her power to keep her job there. Better to encounter Hettie's anger later, when she had got this unpleasant chore over.

To her relief she was able to slip out of the house without awakening her godmother. As she trudged along in the gloomy morning light, the book of ballads in the shoulder-bag she usually carried to work, she had plenty to think about.

Apart from Hettie's stinging remarks to Blane and her emphatic statement that Briony would never work for him again, she had to consider whether Blane was prepared to keep the job open for her. When she arrived at Birchfields would she be met with an abrupt dismissal?

Even if he disregarded Hettie's remarks as too contemptible to be taken seriously, there was still the matter of the book. No amount of patching and smoothing and fixing pages with plastic tape had been able to disguise that it had received very rough treatment indeed.

Briony's brows were furrowed as she continued on

her way. The only bright spot was the mildness of the day. Abergour was enjoying one of those lovely calm autumns which so often happen in the Highlands of Scotland. The trees were a riot of colour, and when she came to the gate of Birchfields she could see the Shetlands in their paddock. The two boys must have pitched in and added the ponies to their own work-loads, for the little animals were obviously well cared for.

As usual she turned towards the tack room, this time half expecting it to be locked, but the door was already open and she wrinkled her nose at the smell that came to meet her. Someone was already making up a mash for a horse.

She entered to find Blane stirring a huge pot on the stove.

He turned and surveyed her. 'So you're back! Fully recovered, I hope!'

He seemed in excellent humour, and Briony, considering Hettie's final speech to him, was taken aback. Had he forgotten that she had been forbidden to return to the Riding School, or did it simply not matter to him what Hettie said?

She decided to reply in an equally casual manner. 'There was really nothing much the matter with me. I stayed in more to satisfy Hettie than anything else—she was so fussed and upset.'

He nodded. 'Yes, I think Hettie's bark is worse than her bite. If you stick to your guns she won't be able to do much about it. After all, you're a big girl now, and capable of making your own decisions.' He turned back to stirring the mash. 'Has a horrible smell, this stuff,' he remarked after a moment, 'but it's just what the doctor ordered—or rather the vet—a nice hot mash with molasses added!'

His words only added to Briony's discomfiture. The picture was only too plain. Not only the two boys had been shouldering her share of the chores, but Blane himself had had to pitch in. But what did it mean? Was this a temporary thing, meant to fill in until her return, or had he decided that the School could very easily dispense with her assistance?

She waited awkwardly and then said, 'I—I suppose it's all right, is it?'

He turned his head. 'All right? What on earth do you mean?'

'I mean, it's all right for me to come back and start again?'

'And why should it not be right for you to come back?'

'Well, I mean, about Hettie——' she began. 'You see, I overheard what she said to you, and—When she's in a bit of a temper she flies out and says anything that comes into her head, and she doesn't seem to understand that I can't sponge on her. She seems to think I could live quite happily with her, without having a job, or earning anything.'

'Yes, your godmother is a very warlike little woman,' he agreed. 'And I must say when she lived here at Birchfields I found her a great trial. But since our last encounter my estimation of her has gone up.'

'What?' Briony could scarcely believe her ears.

'It's true, she told me off in no uncertain manner. But at least this time her remarks made some sense. I could see she had your welfare at heart. She would fight for you like a tiger, if any danger threatened—or rather like a hen for her chick.'

Briony looked at him speechless. This was the very last reaction she had expected from the hot-tempered Blane. Then, at the realisation of what this meant, she drew a deep breath. That Hettie and Blane should ever have the slightest understanding of one another was something she had not dared to hope for.

'And now,' he continued briskly, 'let's take this

opportunity while the mash cools a bit to have a chat. We always seem to be too busy for the social graces, don't we?'

Reluctantly Briony seated herself near the table and he pulled forward a chair on the other side. Now for it, she was thinking. How quickly his affable manner would disappear when he caught sight of his precious book!

But his first words astounded her. 'Well, and how does it feel to be the heroine of the hour?' he demanded.

'What?' she exclaimed, her voice rising in astonishment. At the same time she could not help feeling a certain amount of relief that she was to have a few moments' respite before breaking the news to him.

He regarded her steadily with those amazingly penetrating eyes for a long moment and then said, 'Apparently it hasn't struck you that you made yourself quite ill when you got lost and had to spend most of the night in the quarry when you weren't even properly dressed for the weather. I believe that by giving your jacket and cap to Sandra you saved her life. Apart from that, you kept her spirits up. She knew that help was close at hand and that she would soon be collected. Senga spotted the cap right away.'

At the mention of Senga's name Briony remembered the book of Scottish ballads, so tattered and mudstained. It seemed to be burning a hole in her shoulderbag.

With a sigh she slipped the bag from her shoulder and slowly began to unzip it, thinking as she did so that this approval, which felt like balm to her, would disappear fairly quickly when Blane's eyes fell upon Senga's precious gift. How was she going to break the news to him tactfully? she wondered.

'Something else happened that day,' she began carefully. 'Do you remember you lent me a book of Scottish ballads?'

He nodded. 'Yes, of course.'

'And you told me to take great care of it,' she rushed on a little desperately.

He frowned a little impatiently. 'Yes, I remember. What about it?'

'Well, you see, I had it in my jacket pocket. But I put the jacket round Sandra and——' she pulled out the brown paper wrapping and opened the book out dramatically in front of him, 'this is what happened to it.'

She saw his expression change and the familiar hard glaze seemed to settle on his features. She closed her eyes for a moment. Now for it, she was thinking. She waited shrinking as she anticipated the harsh cold words she knew could so easily overwhelm her with misery.

'Put it away,' he said shortly. 'Don't let me see it ever again.'

With a shaking hand she replaced it in her bag. One thing was clear, and that was that the destruction of the book meant even more to him than she had feared. He must hate her for what she had done.

But when he spoke again he had changed the subject completely. 'I think it's time we made the final preparations for this treasure hunt,' he said. 'Senga tells me the children are eager to have it now. If we delay too long they'll only lose interest. If you feel up to it I wonder if you would help me to choose prizes for the winners. It should be easy to get something suitable in Aberdeen.'

Briony hesitated for an instant. She was already in Senga's bad books. If she were to travel into Aberdeen with him to select prizes for the children, surely Senga would resent it bitterly.

Although the thought of an outing with him made her heart beat a little faster, she said reluctantly, 'I—I don't think I'd better.'

Blane tested the warmth of the mash, then looked up with that swift, keen, assessing glance that she knew so well. 'And why not, may I ask?'

What could she say that would sound convincing? she

wondered. 'Oh, I've so much to do—so much to catch up with after being off. The tack room should be tidied, and——' She stopped, aware that he didn't believe a word she was saying.

'And why should Johnny not do some of the straightening up?' he enquired with an air of feigned surprise. 'After all, that's what I employ him for, apart from his other duties.'

Briony gave a light laugh which, even to her own ears, sounded highly artificial. 'Oh, you know—a woman's touch and all that!'

'Rubbish!' he said curtly. 'And now I don't want any arguments. You're coming to Aberdeen with me and that's that! Unless,' he added suavely, 'you prefer to give in your notice?'

She glanced at him apprehensively. That was the last thing in the world she wanted—to be left helpless again, and living on Hettie's charity. But she knew Blane well enough by now to know that his words were not to be taken lightly.

'Well,' he demanded impatiently. 'Are you, or aren't you?'

'Yes, of course I'll come,' she said.

'Well then, why not let's start off immediately?'

She glanced down at her shabby jeans in dismay. 'But I couldn't possibly go in these clothes,' she told him. 'I'll have to go back to Amulree and change.'

He glanced at his watch. 'All right, but don't be too long. If there's one thing I can't stand, it's hanging around while a woman titivates herself.'

As she hurried towards the cottage Briony felt resentment grow. This wasn't the way he would have treated the soignée Senga, who always looked the height of sophistication. But then, she told herself, her appearance could hardly be of any interest to him. She was only his hired employee, to obey his demands without question.

She found Hettie, trowel in hand, busily gardening as she approached the cottage.

Hettie stood up, her eyes angry. 'You sneaked away this morning before I was up——' she began.

'I'm perfectly all right,' Briony protested. 'And I can't remain an invalid for ever, you know. I simply have to work for my living.'

'So you're back with that man again,' Hettie said bitterly.

'Yes, and very lucky to have my job,' Briony said firmly. 'And now, Hettie, I'll have to rush. He has asked me to go into Aberdeen with him, to pick prizes for the treasure hunt.'

As she saw Hettie open her mouth to object, she hurried along the brick path and ran upstairs.

As she opened the narrow white wardrobe in her room her heart sank. There was no doubt about it, there was no possible chance that she could compete sartorially with the elegant Senga. And she had the unpleasant conviction that, even if her clothes were the smartest and most expensive in the world, she would never achieve Senga's air of sophistication. The village milk-maid, that's me, Briony thought wryly.

She reached down a russet brown dress that brought out the highlights in her hair. It was splashed with a broad zig-zag design of white, and with it she wore white sandals and matching handbag. As she surveyed herself critically in the long mirror on the back of the wardrobe door she decided that a dash of colour was needed. From one of the drawers of the tallboy she took a scarf of bright coral chiffon and tied it in a careless knot to the handles of her handbag.

She hesitated. Should she take a coat? But she had no coat that went well with her outfit, and as the day was as warm as summer she decided not to bother.

When she went downstairs she found Hettie waiting for her, her lips drawn tight in disapproval. 'Why has that man asked you to go with him into Aberdeen?' she began. 'It strikes me as a very strange idea. After all, it's not part of your duties to buy prizes for the children. It seems to me he has a great cheek to think you're at his beck and call, and——'

'I couldn't refuse,' Briony broke in. 'I want to keep this job. Apart from everything else, I like it. It's interesting and——'

'I don't deny that you like being with animals and having an outdoor job,' Hettie conceded. 'But in my opinion there's something more to it than that. If he's as helpless as all that, why doesn't he let Jean McPhee do his shopping for him, instead of choosing a pretty young girl like yourself? It all sounds to me extremely fishy.'

Briony laughed. 'Now, Hettie, that's utterly ridiculous! If you think he's smitten you're completely mistaken. I'm not his type at all. As far as I can see, he's very interested in Senga MacNeil. And she's more than keen on him, I can assure you.'

Hettie put her hands on her hips and surveyed Briony challengingly. 'In that case, why did he not ask her? After all, she's responsible for the children, isn't she?'

'Yes, but all the same I don't think she'd care to go shopping for them,' Briony remarked. 'I mean, it's just not her line of country.'

'Too grand, I expect!' Hettie put in sarcastically. 'So he makes a slave of you! If you'd any pride, Briony, you'd turn him down.'

Briony gave a little moue of resignation. 'I'm afraid when it comes to holding my job I've very little pride,' she admitted. 'Anyway, it will be a change from grooming ponies and teaching children how to ride.'

But Hettie was unappeased. 'All I can say is I've never known a man yet who didn't like to make up to a pretty girl, so whether he's keen on Senga MacNeil or not is beside the question. You just watch out for yourself this afternoon, that's all!'

Briony was hurrying towards Birchfields when she encountered Johnny exercising one of Blane's thoroughbreds. When Johnny reined him in he danced nervously on the grass verge. 'Watch out,' Johnny called. 'We don't want you falling into the ditch just when you're all dolled up. You've certainly come around all right! But why the smart outfit?'

'I'm going into Aberdeen with the boss. He doesn't feel he's up to choosing the right prizes for the children—and frankly, I don't think he is either. Anyway, I'm delighted to get the chance of the afternoon off instead of slopping around in shabby old jeans and scuffed sweaters that have been washed too often.'

He leaned forward and gazed down at her, his eyes twinkling. 'Oh, come, Briony, don't try to pull the wool over my eyes—you look positively glowing. I always knew you'd fall for the boss. Women always do,' he ended with a sigh.

CHAPTER TEN

WHEN she arrived at Birchfields, Blane was waiting for her by the big pale grey car. He was wearing a suit of fine tweed that showed off his blocky build, with a matching cap jauntily perched at an angle over his eyes.

For the first time it struck her that, while he could not be called handsome, he was not the kind of man one would pass in a crowd without a second glance. His rugged face, with those strikingly acute blue eyes, was full of interest and energy, and vitality seemed to crackle from him like live electricity.

Briony caught the quick sideways flickering glance of his blue eyes as she slipped into her place beside him and realised that it had encompassed every detail of her outfit. Somewhere, deep down, she felt a little glow of satisfaction. Without making any remark, he had noted and approved of her appearance.

As they set off she could not resist a little covert glance at his profile—her reactions heightened by Johnny's recent remarks. But his rugged features betrayed nothing except concentration on controlling the powerful car.

As they drove through the magically beautiful countryside Blane's mood seemed to soften, and she was surprised at his deep knowledge of the legends and stories of the district. Knowing that Byron was her favourite poet, he told her that Byron had spent his childhood in Aberdeen, and she saw how this rugged granite background seemed to be a suitable setting for the author of the haunting 'Dark Lochnagar'.

As they chatted Briony felt relaxed and at ease, and it struck her that it was the first time she had not felt

135

defensive and on edge in Blane's presence. Perhaps it was because on this occasion she no longer regarded him as her boss who seemed to have eyes in the back of his head.

As soon as they reached Aberdeen he drove her on a short tour of the city. He pointed out the Brig of Balgowrie and told her that, as a child, Byron used to be terrified when he rode across it on his pony because it had been foretold that a widow's only son would come to disaster there and he feared that this prophecy referred to him.

There had been a brief shower as they approached the city and the old buildings sparkled in the sunshine. Against this in contrast were the great blocks of high-rise flats looking incongruously modern againt the ancient stone.

Curiously enough, up till now, Briony had not given any thought to Jeremy, and it was only as they drove past the imposing façade of Stanton Hodges and Company that there flooded into her mind the memory of that disastrous interview with Jeremy and the bitterness she had felt at his rejection. As her eyes riveted on the cold gleam of the plate glass windows she wondered behind which one Jeremy worked. Was he seated behind the successful businessman's immense desk, or even, she thought with a pang, chatting with the elegant Texan girl.

She jerked her head away and stared ahead. She mustn't think of the past, she told herself, not now when her life was set on a different path.

They stopped at a traffic light, and she became aware that Blane's eyes were fixed on her.

'How long is it since you've seen anything of Aberdeen?' he asked quietly, and she wondered for a moment if he had noticed her unhappiness.

'Oh, I used to come here on trips when I was staying with Hettie at Birchfields as a child.' She tried to force a smile. 'But I'm afraid the only thing I took an interest in was the wonderful teas with luscious cream cakes we used to indulge in when the shopping expedition was over.'

The lights had changed and they drove on. To her relief then Blane relapsed into silence. Not for worlds would she want him to know of that awful debacle with Jeremy!

'I suppose it's time we got down to it and chose the trinkets for the children,' he was saying, as they drove along Union Street.

When he had parked, they retraced their steps, pausing now and then to gaze into the windows of jewellers' shops. Briony enjoyed herself thoroughly. There was something exhilarating about the sparkle and glitter.

'Well, what do you think?' Blane asked.

'What about a charm bracelet?' she ventured, 'with identical charms for a beginning—say a tiny stirrup. Later on, the children's parents or relations or friends might add to their collection at birthdays and Christmas and so on.'

Blane looked at her doubtfully. 'Perhaps we'd better go in and see what they have to offer, before making up our minds.'

Once inside, they separated and examined the showcases. Briony found herself fascinated by one in particular. It contained trays of engagement rings in every conceivable gem. They shimmered and flared in the cunningly positioned lighting. Not far from her she saw a couple, their heads close together as they discussed the rings in one of the cases. The expression on their faces made it very obvious that they were oblivious of the impression they made as, hand in hand, they gazed down on the glittering jewels.

For a moment Briony let her mind wander. Suppose, instead of coming to buy trinkets for the girls, she and Blane were on a different mission—to purchase the ring she preferred to all the others. It was composed of sap-

phires the colour of the night sky and diamonds as
bright as the stars. As her eyes lingered on it an assistant
approached. And at the same time Blane joined her.

'Interested in engagement rings?' the assistant
enquired with the faintly sly expression the elderly are
inclined to reserve for engaged couples.

Briony felt herself blush furiously. 'Oh no, of course
not!' she muttered. Then, turning to Blane, she said
rapidly and with rather too much interest, 'Well, have
you seen anything you would like for the children?'

He shook his head. 'No, I'm afraid selecting trinkets
for little girls is distinctly not my forte. But I did see a
display case over here that might contain something you
would think suitable.'

As she followed him she had the distinct impression
that she had detected a sardonic gleam in his eyes.
Could he by any chance have divined the thoughts that
had been running through her mind as she gazed at
those opulent engagement rings? But then how on earth
could he? she thought. The idea was utterly ridiculous!
Yet, in spite of his rugged, rough exterior she had
always subconsciously known that he was acutely per-
ceptive. She would have to be a bit more cautious when
she let her mind wander in Blane's direction, she told
herself.

Briony now found herself in front of a case which
held such a wealth of suitable gifts that she felt at a loss.
Here was a multitude of trinkets to gladden any child's
heart; necklaces of coral, tiny animals fashioned in mar-
casite, owls with topaz eyes, slender silver bangles, a
variety of charms in gold and silver. In the end she was
divided between a brooch fashioned like a Scottish
thistle, made of amethyst chips from the Cairngorm
mountains, and one representing a spray of lucky white
heather, the blossoms formed of tiny seed pearls.

'Well, what do you think?' Blane asked at last.

Briony frowned thoughtfully. 'I don't know which

I prefer, the amethyst brooch or the Scottish white heather.'

'Well, why not get one of each?' he asked.

Briony smiled. 'That wouldn't do at all! Can you imagine the squabbles there would be if they both wanted the same brooch!'

'Well, I did tell you I didn't understand the mentality of young females,' he said, his mouth quirking.

'I think on the whole I'll plump for the thistle,' Briony decided. 'I've the feeling these brooches will get some pretty rough handling, and the thistles look more durable than the seed pearls.'

When the trinkets had been wrapped in cotton wool, and tied up in separate boxes, Briony tucked them into her handbag.

As they went out into the street, Blane said with relief, 'Well, that's over! But now there's the question of consolation prizes.'

'You mean you're going to give them *all* something?' Briony asked in surprise.

'Why not? I know this much about the kids, they've no competitive spirit. It will cause bad feeling if they don't go home with something. And what's more,' he added with a grin, 'I'll get the reputation of being a skinflint—and that won't do the Lennox Riding School any good.'

She smiled, then said severely, 'Now you're being cynical!'

'And isn't that what you've always thought of me?' And for a moment he looked at her directly, his eyes grave.

Briony evaded his glance. There was something all-encompassing about it that made her feel uncomfortable. 'What were you thinking of getting for the others?' she asked hurriedly.

'I suppose sweets would be in order,' he said in his usual brisk, decisive manner. 'That's usually what they give at these affairs. These trinkets of ours will be quite an innovation. We want it to be a roaring success, don't we?'

She nodded, feeling her heart sink a little. Yes, he wanted this treasure hunt to be a success—for Senga's sake. It would give her a good image with Miss Anderson, and justify the riding lessons and other expenses that had been involved.

Quickly Blane chose one of the largest confectioners in Union Street. Briony was amazed at the prices of some of the goods. Here were gigantic boxes of sweets at fantastic prices. There were hand-made chocolates from the Continent, and all sorts of mouthwatering dainties. 'How on earth could anyone afford this?' she gasped as she gazed around her.

'Money is no object in Aberdeen now,' he told her. 'The worst paid workers in the oil-fields earn hundreds of pounds per week. Anything they fancy, they can have.'

After some searching Briony managed to collect a selection of small boxes of chocolates with attractively coloured pictures on the lids. When these had been packed into a large cardboard container, Blane carried it out to the car and locked it safely in the trunk.

'And now,' he remarked, 'I think it's time we had something to eat.' He glanced at his watch. 'But first I have a bit of business to do.' He pointed out a hotel. 'If we went along there now would you mind waiting for a little while? I shan't be long.'

'I'd rather do a little window-shopping,' she told him diffidently. 'Aberdeen has changed so completely from the town I knew when I was a child, and the windows are so exciting. It's wonderful to gaze at such expensive things, even if I can't afford them.'

'Suit yourself!' he told her. 'I'm just as pleased you've decided to do this, in case I'm delayed. But if I am, go in and wait for me in the foyer. But I'll try not to be too long.'

Later on, as she leisurely made her way along Aberdeen's principal street, Briony marvelled anew at the shop-window displays. There were so many things to cater for the wealth that had flowed in since the beginning of the oil boom. Certain shops were completely given over to American delicacies. Another contained a display of the most expensive sweaters she had ever seen. Each one was unique and knitted from the finest wools. She marvelled at some of the designs—snowy mountains or calm seas with sailing boats, and one particularly clever one actually showed a vista of a street complete with pedestrians. Each sweater was totally different, never to be repeated and somewhat resembling a painting. Briony sighed enviously. Evidently, to many people in Aberdeen money meant nothing, and she had no doubt that these fabulously priced goods would find ready buyers.

Time passed quickly as she made her odyssey from shop to shop, not daring to buy more than a few toilet requisites, although her heart yearned for some of the luxuries that were being so temptingly displayed.

She glanced at her watch. It was time she stopped dawdling and moved on to the hotel, she decided. Blane Lennox, she knew from experience, was not a man who would wait patiently.

It was as she was approaching the entrance to the hotel that she felt her heart give a thud of recognition, for the figure that was approaching her was Jeremy's. At the first glance she saw that he had not changed in the slightest. He was as handsomely fair as ever. But she was a different person now, with a completely altered outlook on life. A new Briony—much more experienced!

Jeremy's rejection had left its scar on her heart, she realised. Never again would she respond so eagerly to a man's profession of love. For her there would never be another springtime, she thought bitterly.

For a moment she had the satisfaction of seeing the disconcerted look that flitted across his handsome face as he caught sight of her.

But almost at once it was replaced by the glowing smile that, in other days, would have made her heart beat quickly. 'Why, Briony, what on earth are you doing here? I thought——' He stopped awkwardly.

Yes, you thought I'd gone home with my tail between my legs, Briony thought. He was so sure of his attractions then that the idea that she should remain and seek out a new life had not even occurred to him.

'I've got a job in Abergour,' she told him shortly.

'You've taken a job?' he asked, surprised. 'But what sort of a job would you get in a place like Abergour? As far as I know, it's in the wilds.'

'I'm working for a man who bought my godmother's place and he's running it as a riding school, and I like the work very much,' she told him. 'I always wanted an outdoor life anyway, so it suits me very well.'

There was a pause while he scanned her face intently. Was he looking for signs of a broken heart? she wondered wryly. Did he by any chance think she was putting on a false front to hide her hurt at his rejection?

Well, whatever he was searching for he didn't get, she thought with a little glow of satisfaction as she detected a faint look of disappointment flit over his face.

When he had once more repeated how delighted he was to see her, and showed no signs of breaking off the conversation, the suspicion flashed through her mind that the affair with the American girl was over and that he was now attempting to patch things up, and renew his relationship with her.

A moment later he made it clear her surmise was all too correct. She had hit the nail on the head. With the disarming impulsiveness he could assume when he wanted to be at his most charming, Jeremy tucked her arm in his and pressed it close. 'But this is wonderful! I can't tell you how bucked I feel meeting you again. What about some coffee and a chat?' He half turned as though to lead her into the hotel.

She pulled her arm away abruptly. 'Thanks, no! I'm to meet someone.'

He looked dismayed. 'Then you'll have time for a drink.'

'No, Jeremy,' she replied firmly. 'There would be no point in it. After all, what have you and I to chat about? As far as I'm concerned the past is over.'

But Jeremy was not to be so easily put off. 'There's no reason why you and I shouldn't be friends,' he insisted stubbornly. 'Let's go in for a few minutes. There's something I want to say to you, and I can't do it out here.'

And before she knew quite what had happened Briony found herself hustled willy-nilly into the hotel and plumped down on one of the comfortable blue and green banquettes that lined the foyer.

Briony looked at him in desperation. 'What on earth do you want to talk about, Jeremy?' She glanced anxiously at her watch. Blane would be appearing at any moment and Jeremy was the last person she wanted him to see her with. Nothing would escape his quick eye. Instantly he would be ferreting out the facts behind her humiliating rejection. The thought made her voice shrill with anxiety. 'But this is ridiculous! You made it quite clear the last time we met just how you felt about me.'

'I won't keep you more than a few minutes,' Jeremy assured her hurriedly, with a new air of humility that she had never noticed in him before. 'It's just this, to put it in a nutshell, well—after you'd gone, I realised what a fool I'd been. I must have been crazy to let you go. There were a lot of things I didn't understand. My values are completely different now.' His eyes fixed on her face with new awareness. 'And you know, you're even prettier now than you were—if that's possible.'

Catching a glimpse of herself in the ornate mirror that covered the wall on the opposite side of the foyer, Briony realised he was only speaking the truth. She had new colour in her cheeks and an air of energy and vitality that she had never had when working for Stanton, Hodges & Co. Her hair was rippling and shining, her skin clear and translucent. And, in a strange way, unpredictable as Blane was, she felt more security in her job. Looking back, she realised that she had subconsciously known that her relationship with Jeremy rested on a shaky basis. His facile charm had varied from day to day, and she had never quite known where she was with him. His final departure to Aberdeen and his rejection of her was simply something she had been vaguely dreading since she had first fallen in love with him.

'I take it, then, that it's all over between you and Miss Morgan?' she asked dryly.

'Yes, it's completely all over,' he said eagerly. 'I don't know what on earth made me fall for her in the first place. She's so utterly superficial.'

But Briony was not deceived. 'I think I know how it happened,' she told him. 'She was so sophisticated, a woman of the world, and compared to her I was like the girl next door. All the same, I'd be interested to know why you think she's superficial.'

He had the grace to look faintly abashed. 'Oh, I discovered there's only one thing that interests her, and that's money and position. When the son of a big shot in the oil world blew in from Texas, poor old Jeremy found himself out in the cold. But don't let's talk about the past,' he continued urgently. 'What do you say to my slipping down to Abergour one of these days? We could have a little get-together, just like old times. Don't say no, Briony, because you and I always got on well together, and I do honestly feel rotten about the way I treated you.'

She shook her head and stood up. 'No, Jeremy, it

wouldn't work out. You'd better realise it's all over between us, once and for all.'

Reluctantly he got to his feet. She saw the familiar sulky frown as he realised that his charm was of no avail, and she felt a sense of surprise as she remembered how anxiously she would at one time have tried to avoid his sudden fits of displeasure.

'Very well,' he told her huffily, 'if that's how you feel! But there's no need to be so bitter. After all, we did have some good times together.'

'I'm not bitter,' she assured him. 'Just a bit more wary, perhaps.' But even as she said it she had the guilty feeling that she was not being absolutely honest with him. If Blane had not entered her life would she have rejected Jeremy's attempts at a reconciliation quite so firmly?

'You must give me your address in Abergour,' he urged. 'After all, there is a bond between us, in spite of everything. I've still got your ring, you know. I'll never part from it.'

Reluctantly she did as he asked, and when he had noted down her address, he turned away with that little-boy-wronged air which was, she realised now, part of his stock in trade.

As he left her, she noticed with dismay that Blane had come through the swing doors of the hotel. As he advanced towards her she knew from his expression that he had seen them in conversation, and as Jeremy passed him he turned his head and gave him a searching glance.

'You've fallen in with an acquaintance, I see,' Blane remarked casually as he joined her, and together they moved out of the foyer.

'Oh yes,' she said, trying to sound equally casual. 'Someone who used to work with me in the office!'

'I see! Well, considering I'm later than I expected, it must have helped to pass the time for you.' But the glance he gave her was every bit as searching as the one he had given Jeremy, and she turned her head away with a sudden inexplicable feeling of embarrassment.

To her relief he made no further reference to the incident but chatted easily while they had their meal in the large restaurant. But as far as Briony was concerned, the pleasant companionable relationship which had existed during the drive into town had now evaporated. She felt curiously upset by that chance encounter with Jeremy. The old life had intruded on the new and, in spite of the fact that she had given Jeremy no hope of a reconciliation, there vividly flashed through her mind remembrances of the time when he had meant so much to her—days when she had waited for the phone calls which he had not troubled to make, or had watched the post for letters which had not arrived.

Suddenly she became conscious of the long pause in the conversation and looked up to find Blane's eyes fixed on her troubled face. 'This young friend of yours, he seems a nice enough chap,' he said.

'Oh yes,' she agreed quickly, then found herself babbling on. 'He was always frightfully ambitious, a real go-ahead type, and when the office was opened in Aberdeen he was one of the first to apply to be transferred. I expect he'll wind up an executive in the firm.'

'You didn't mind his going, then?' he asked.

'Why should I?' she replied quickly—rather too quickly, she realised.

He raised his brows 'Don't tell me you're unaware that your friend is extremely good-looking and, I suspect, very charming when he wants to be?'

'No, of course not!' she said airily. 'Jeremy Warne was considered quite a catch. In fact, most of the girls were crazy about him.'

'In that case,' he said dryly, 'he must have left behind quite a lot of broken hearts—with the exception of yours, of course!'

'What on earth do you mean?' she demanded.

'Well, you're obviously not one of the girls he left behind him,' he told her dryly. 'Abergour isn't so far from Aberdeen, after all. You'll have plenty of opportunities for rendezvousing.'

'Considering I spend so much of my time at the Lennox Riding School, working like a slave, I certainly won't have much opportunity to see him,' she replied tartly.

His eyes lit up with amusement and she realised she had hit the right note. Blane Lennox was the sort of man who liked a girl to speak up for herself, and her reply had completely disarmed him—for the time being at least.

But as they strolled towards the car he was silent, and she wondered if it could be possible that he was resentful of her meeting with Jeremy. But she dismissed the thought immediately. Blane had so much self-confidence that the idea of his resenting her interest in another man was ridiculous. Anyway, it was only too clear that Senga was the girl he was interested in!

The reason for his attitude became apparent as they drove swiftly towards Abergour. 'You know, Briony, I wonder how long you're going to be content at the Riding School?'

'What on earth do you mean?' She turned to gaze at him in amazement.

'Well, you've not very many young people to turn to, have you? Oh, you hit it off well enough with the boys, Johnny and Andy: you always seem to have something to laugh and chat about. Now there's this chap in Aberdeen! To begin with, he's more your age than I am, but apart from that, I expect he's good company. It's natural you should get along well. As for me—well, I'm too wrapped up in business perhaps. I never seem to have time to relax. I expect it's because I took on responsibility while I was still very young.'

Briony's first reaction was one of relief. So he suspected nothing more in her relationship with Jeremy than that they had been good pals in her previous job. Somehow she shrank from the thought of his knowing how deeply she had been involved with Jeremy at one time. The story of her humiliating rejection was the last thing she wanted to come to his ears.

She gave him a covert glance. He drove swiftly and expertly, she realised, his eyes fixed on the road, dark and withdrawn. Suddenly she felt a tenderness well up in her heart for him. Strange to think that this stern man should envy the sound of the laughter she shared with Johnny and Andy many a time in the tack room. She could hardly let him know that, since meeting him, Jeremy's facile charm and the fascination that he had once exerted over her had quite faded. And as for Johnny and Andy, as far as she was concerned, they were mere babies! Never at any time had she even remotely thought of taking them seriously.

Well, at any rate, better he should think that what she desired was youthful companionship, than suspect the thrill of happiness she felt when sitting side by side with this vital, mature man who held an attraction for her that frightened her with its intensity.

What would be his reaction, she wondered a little wildly, if she were to tell him now that he was the most fascinating man she had ever met and that she was madly in love with him? To her dismay she heard herself give a little hysterical giggle.

He glanced at her. 'What's the joke?'

'Oh, just thinking of something utterly ludicrous,' she told him.

His lips curved in a smile that, to her surprise, was almost tender. 'Well, at any rate you seem to have enjoyed our little outing.'

'Yes, of course I have,' she told him truthfully. Not even Jeremy could spoil this for her, she thought, and it was something she could remember in future days, when this hard taskmaster of hers brought her temper to boiling point.

In companionable silence ''ey drove through the village and finally stopped outside the little wooden gate to Amulree Cottage.

CHAPTER ELEVEN

As the car stopped, Briony said, 'I'll change into working gear and come along for the rest of the afternoon. I shan't be long.'

'No need to do that,' Blane replied. 'You've done well enough for one day as far as I'm concerned.'

She hesitated before getting out of the car. How she longed to be able to prolong the occasion by inviting him into Amulree for tea! But Hettie's antagonistic attitude towards him made such a thing completely out of the question.

Reluctantly she reached for the door, but her hand had barely touched it when Blane enclosed her fingers in a firm grip that prevented her from pulling on the handle.

Startled, she turned to face him.

'No need to go right away, Briony.' His voice was low and urgent and something in the steady, almost fierce look that raked her face made her heart beat faster.

'Hettie will be wondering why——' she began.

'Let's keep Hettie out of this. Would you be so anxious to part from me if I were Jeremy Warne, I wonder?'

'But that's nonsense!' she said, attempting a laugh which, even to her own ears, sounded nervously uncertain.

'You mean you've never as much as exchanged a parting kiss?' he asked sardonically.

'What do you mean by that?'

'Look, you can't pull the wool over my eyes, Briony. I've seen you and this Jeremy together. Don't tell me you've not been very close friends!'

She attempted a show of indifference. 'But of course we have! I've told you that we worked together in the same office. People can't meet day after day and remain strangers. Naturally we got to know each other well.'

'How well?' he rapped, his eyes steely.

She turned her head away, as she realised with a rush that whatever feeling she had once had for Jeremy was nothing like the overwhelming attraction she felt for this man so close beside her.

But before she could gather her wits to form a suitable answer, his arms were about her. 'Dear Briony, can't you see I don't want you to leave me—ever,' he said, his voice very low, as his lips met hers.

It was then, with dizzying happiness, she realised that she had been right, for never in Jeremy's arms had she felt such ecstasy.

She was breathless when he released her. But as her head stopped whirling, a cold monitoring little voice seemed to whisper a warning in her ear, reminding her that Jeremy had caused her heartbreak. How much more so would it be with a man like Blane, were she fool enough to fall for what was probably, as far as he was concerned, no more than a moment's indulgence. To him, this couldn't mean anything serious or lasting, when it was obvious that he had his future pretty well mapped out with Senga.

Well, this time she was not going to be a dupe, she told herself with sudden overriding fury. Never again would a man attract her and then discard her as casually as Jeremy had done! And before she realised just what she was about, she had struck out wildly at Blane—ineffectually, as it proved, for in her rage, her fingers barely grazed his jaw.

She didn't wait to see his reaction, but wrenching at the car door, she sprang out and raced up the path. But as she pushed on the cottage door, she found that it was locked. Hettie must be out. Tremulous with agitation, she fumbled in her bag for her key. As she did so, she heard Blane's car roar off, scattering gravel that spurted beneath the wheels like an expression of his anger and contempt.

Sick at heart, she went into the sitting-room. It was a consolation that Hettie was not at home, she thought drearily. She would not, at least, have to face her god-mother's reproaches had she been a witness to the scene.

Wearily she climbed the steps to her room and sank down on her bed. Her thoughts whirled round and round in confusion. Why on earth had she acted so impulsively? If only she had retained her dignity and, instead of letting emotion overwhelm her, had dismissed the episode with the sort of sophistication Senga would have shown. Instead, she had reacted impulsively. He would bitterly resent her behaviour—of that she was certain. So proud a man would not take that treatment without retaliating, and she dreaded facing him in the morning.

On the following day Briony lingered over her breakfast, reluctant to face the walk to Birchfields and the moment of encountering him. It would be like confronting a dragon in his den, she decided apprehensively.

Hettie glanced at her curiously, as she bustled around collecting the ingredients for her weekly bread-making session. 'It's not like you to dawdle over breakfast. Usually you can't get up to Birchfields fast enough! Not that it would be any harm if you lost that precious job of yours!'

With a guilty start Briony got to her feet. It was true that she was reluctant to leave the familiar and sheltering walls of Amulree. But Hettie was beginning to clear away the breakfast table in such a marked manner that Briony realised she would have to set off.

As she approached the Riding School she seemed to

be seeing it with fresh eyes. Smooth green turf enclosed by gleaming white railings; severely symmetrical loose-boxes—it occurred to her that this new Birchfields that Blane had created was strictly functional. Even the flower-beds in front of the house seemed regimented. No doubt he would consider a brightly coloured herbaceous border a waste of valuable space!

At the moment there was no sign of him, and as she walked along the drive she wondered if she could slip into the tack room without encountering him.

But she was out of luck. As she went into the yard she saw him approach and to her dismay she realised that things were much worse than she had expected. Instead of looking irate, he looked dangerously calm, his face set, as though carved out of hard stone, his eyes cold.

'You're late!' he said shortly, his voice full of contempt, and to her dismay Briony felt her cheeks redden.

She was trying to think of a reply that would be conciliating without sounding too apologetic, when he said abruptly, 'Well, don't stand around. Get cracking! There's plenty of work for you to do this morning. First of all, I think you'd better start and muck out the stables.'

She glanced at him in surprise. Usually the lads did this job as a matter of course, and, without thinking, she blurted out, 'But the boys usually do that!'

'Well, you're doing it this morning! What the boys usually do has nothing to do with the matter,' he replied grimly. 'When I engaged you it was on the understanding that you would be a capable stable-hand. Now, it seems, you're too grand to sully your dainty fingers by mucking out.'

'No, of course not,' she said hastily. 'I don't mind doing it at all, if that's what you want.'

'That's exactly what I want!' he told her dryly. 'But

if at any time you feel incapable of carrying out the ordinary duties of a stable lad, just let me know, and I certainly shan't hold you against your will!'

She had finished and was leaning a little wearily against the half door of the last loose-box when he approached again. Had he been watching her, and timed his visit almost to the exact minute when she would have completed her task?

When he had inspected the work he turned and stared at her remotely. 'I suggest now that you clean the tack. I want it washed and thoroughly saddle-soaped. It seems to me that Johnny and Andy have been skimping on the job, but I have the feeling that you'll prove more conscientious.'

His voice still held its dry ironic tone. But the idea that she should spend a boring session in the tack room instead of attending to her beloved Shetlands filled her with rebellious dismay.

'But what about the ponies?' she asked quickly.

'It's about time you realised that you're not going to get all the cushy jobs here,' he told her brusquely, as he left her.

Briony stared after him, her mouth set mulishly. She wasn't sorry now, she decided, that she had behaved as she had done on the previous evening. Blane had had it coming to him! And as for her getting the cushy jobs— how typical of the man! She had done nothing but work her fingers to the bone since she had come to Birchfields.

But she'd show him, she told herself firmly, as she walked towards the tack room. Never again would she give him the slightest assistance over and above her ordinary duties. She'd leave his beastly tack room glittering like the sun, she told herself, but not one finger would she lift for him apart from that. In future she would treat him with cold aloofness, she thought with a certain amount of satisfaction. Let him organise the treasure hunt himself, if he wanted to, or, better still, let Senga organise it for him!

But even as she realised that this was most probably what he would do, she felt cold fingers clutch at her heart. She had enjoyed working on the treasure hunt with Blane. The idea of Senga taking her place as his assistant, with all the intimacy it implied, filled her with gloom.

She set to work right away on the monotonous business of examining each piece of tack; washing and polishing the leather until it gleamed, and the buckles until they glittered. She missed the company of the two boys. Usually when they were there they kept the rather battered transistor going at full pelt. Now she worked in silence, only her frustration giving speed to her fingers.

She was still at it when the boys came in for their morning break, and soon it was clear that Johnny too was not in the best of humours. He was particularly vitriolic concerning Blane's Hanoverian. 'That animal is a proper devil,' he said, disgruntled. 'You don't know what trouble I had trying to handle him this morning, and I'd no sooner finished with him than I had to see to the Shetlands. The boss has given them to me—and mind you, that's something I hadn't bargained for.'

Briony could feel her cheeks grow pale. 'You mean you're to take care of them in future?'

'Yes, the little darlings are all mine from now on,' Johnny replied grumpily. It was plain it was a task that was not at all welcome. 'What on earth has happened between you and the boss? I could see he was doing it just to spite you, because he knows how keen you are on the little fellows. You must have rubbed him up the wrong way on that trip to Aberdeen and, believe me, he's taking it out on Andy and myself in no small measure.' He glanced towards Andy for confirmation.

Andy, who was never very talkative, nodded dolefully.

The two boys stared at her enquiringly and Briony put on a great show of applying metal polish to a buckle. Her head bent, she rubbed vigorously.

During the following days the tension didn't ease up. Each morning when she arrived, Blane managed to select for her the most disagreeable jobs he could think up, and what was more, managed to provide her with another task as soon as she had completed the first.

The boys were unnaturally subdued as they went about their work, keeping a wary eye out for trouble and avoiding encounters with their employer as much as possible. Briony became aware that their attitude towards her had changed subtly. There was very little chatting now at the tea-breaks and even the transistor was toned down, as though they were afraid its cheerful sound might bring down Blane's wrath on them. It was clear they were holding her entirely responsible for Blane's irascibility.

A few days later as they lounged in the tack room moodily munching sandwiches washed down by steaming mugs of strong tea, she burst out irritably, 'I wish you two wouldn't put all the blame on me! After all, he may have quarrelled with Senga, and is simply letting off steam on us!'

Johnny refilled his mug and shook his head decisively. 'No, it's not Senga. I've kept an eye on him when she brings the kids down from the school. But they seem to be as thick as thieves. Great pals, like they always were!'

Briony felt her heart sink. Yes, it was true. Senga with her ready wit was the only person who could bring a smile to Blane's grimly set features.

By her silly behaviour that evening after their jaunt to Aberdeen she had as good as thrown Senga into his arms. How naïve she had been! But then she had always found it difficult to hide her feelings, and it would be too late to begin now, she suspected with a sigh.

Johnny had begun to speak to Andy, his voice a background to her thoughts. Suddenly she became aware that he was saying, 'It doesn't look as if there'll be a present from the boss this time.'

'Present?' she queried. 'Why should he give you a present?'

'For his birthday, the day after tomorrow,' Andy put in. 'Ever since we began to work here the boss has remembered our birthdays. It looks like this time Johnny is going to be out of luck.'

It was on the tip of Briony's tongue to ask what shape Blane's remembrance took when, as though guessing her interest, Johnny said with a grin, 'He doesn't give a birthday party, you understand.'

The idea seemed to both boys to be so completely ludicrous that they burst into laughter.

'But he usually gives a cheque, and very welcome it is too!' Johnny ended.

'No, there's no use wishing for that this year,' Andy told him with his usual solemnity.

Johnny's face fell as he laid down his mug. 'Well, that's that! I suppose I'd better get back to work and not hope for anything.'

The two boys left the tack room in silence.

If only she were back in their good graces Blane's ostracism might be a little more endurable, Briony thought, as she washed up the mugs and replaced them on their shelf. Then an idea struck her. Why shouldn't she give a birthday party for Johnny? After all, she wasn't the high-and-mighty Blane Lennox. And even if the boys thought it unusual, they would put it down to inexperience, and she had the feeling they would most probably thoroughly enjoy it.

She would make sausage rolls, she decided. That would be the sort of feast Johnny and Andy would enjoy. With chocolate mousse to follow. Johnny had often said it was his favourite sweet. Perhaps too, she thought, growing ambitious, one of those special iced cakes which Annie kept in cardboard boxes, just in case one of her customers might have a birthday coming up!

Annie could still be glimpsed in her inner shop as Briony was going home that evening, and as she made her purchases she could see Annie's eyes quicken with interest.

'So you're going to have a party! Now whose birthday could it be? Not Hettie's, I know, because hers isn't for a couple of months yet!' Annie queried as she parcelled up the pink and white iced cake. 'It's lucky for you I've got a couple of pounds of frozen pastry left. Now which will you have, puff or short—although there's nothing like the home-made stuff, if you ask me.'

Briony nodded placatingly. 'I suppose so, but I'm afraid I'm not very good at making it. The puff never seems to rise and the short's much too hard.'

Annie sniffed. 'That's what's wrong with the younger generation. Everything's done for them. In my young day now——' And she went into one of her rigmaroles about the good old days.

After the evening meal, when Hettie had taken out her electric sewing machine and started sewing, Briony went into the kitchen and began to assemble the materials she had purchased from Annie Skinner.

The door between the two rooms was open and Hettie switched off her machine to ask, 'And now what are you about?'

'I'm going to try to make sausage rolls,' Briony told her. 'It's for Johnny Howie's birthday. I'm going to have a little party for him during the morning break. It's the day after tomorrow, so I thought I'd better get started now.'

Hettie nodded approvingly. 'That's something I'm glad to hear. He's a nice bright boy, and he doesn't get much pleasure in his life, what with his mother being an invalid. Well, it's good to hear someone's taking an interest in him, for I can't see Blane Lennox being particularly worried about whether he has a birthday celebration or not.'

Briony began to roll out the pastry. Then, without stopping to think, she said, 'Yes, I'm afraid you're right. Blane Lennox is in a black mood these days. But it's not only with Johnny—he's out with all of us.'

'Aha, so you're beginning to see through him, are you?' exclaimed Hettie. 'You're getting a taste of the real Blane Lennox at last!'

For a few minutes Briony worked in silence. 'Tell me, Hettie,' she said at last, 'why is it you dislike him? It seems to me that fixing up the flat for you was an extraordinarily generous thing to do.'

For a moment Hettie seemed taken aback and even faintly embarrassed. 'I see, so he's told you about the flat, has he?'

'Yes, and he showed it to me. I must say it looked like a perfect little jewel. If I'd been in your place I'd have been thrilled to bits.'

'Oh, you would, would you!' Hettie rejoined, switching on her machine again and stitching furiously. But at the end of the seam she switched off again to say, 'It just so happens that I left because I had to. Oh, I know it sounds very generous, very bighearted, his equipping the flat for me, but that's how he wanted it to sound, so that his neighbours would have a good opinion of him. But he had no intention of letting me stay there—not even from the first!'

'You mean, he actually told you to leave?' Briony asked slowly.

Hettie sniffed. 'Oh, not in so many words. He's too smart for that, is Mr Blane Lennox! But he got that housekeeper of his, that Jean McPhee, to do his dirty work for him. Why, the way that woman spoke to me— I shan't forget it till my dying day.'

'Are you sure?' Briony asked frowningly. Somehow

this did not sound at all characteristic of Blane. To get his housekeeper to act for him did not seem the sort of thing he would do.

'Well, perhaps he didn't exactly put her up to it,' Hettie said grudgingly, 'but he should have kept her in her place, instead of letting her say anything she likes.'

Briony sighed and returned to her cooking once more. But Hettie's words lingered uncomfortably in her mind. If Blane intended to marry Senga he would realise that she would hardly tolerate the interfering Hettie sharing Birchfields. Could her godmother have hit on the truth, and had Blane, in his usual autocratic way, decided to get rid of her?

'Now look what I've done!' Hettie switched off the machine in exasperation. 'I'm so upset I've done this seam all squinty. You know, Briony, I could cook up those sausage rolls in a twinkle, if you'd unpick this seam for me.'

Although she did not relish the thought of unpicking the seam, Briony saw that Hettie was too upset to continue sewing and that she'd much rather have a go at the sausage rolls. She laid down the rolling-pin, washed her hands, and goodnaturedly took up the scissors and began to unpick the seam.

'The oven's not hot enough,' Hettie told her reprimandingly, as she turned the switch higher. 'And why on earth did you get puff pastry?'

Briony sighed. 'I thought perhaps the boys might like it better.'

There was a short pause while Hettie expertly greased a baking tray. Then she said, with an air of casualness that didn't deceive Briony, 'You know, I've been thinking about you and I've been wondering if there's any chance you might take up with that fellow in Aberdeen.'

'What?' Briony glanced up in amazement.

'You're very young. And after all, couples have their

differences—especially when they're engaged. That's the time for quarrels and arguments, but after a while they resolve their problems and often things turn out right for them in the end. Wouldn't it be a good idea to get in touch with him? After all, he's not so far away now, and the main thing is that he's nearer your own age, and that can be very important, you know.'

So Hettie was back to the consideration that Blane was older than she was! But that was part of the attraction he had for her. He made men like Jeremy seem immature and, in fact—Briony had to admit to herself—boring.

'And it's not only that Blane Lennox is older than you are—he's devious too. It's just that you're too young to realise that. You haven't had enough experience of men.'

'I can't see what difference it makes,' Briony said wearily, 'considering he has every intention of marrying Senga MacNeil. And no doubt she'll be mature enough to deal with him,' she added ironically.

But she was thinking that Hettie showed herself a very poor judge of character. On the contrary, an overpowering directness and almost brutal tactlessness was Blane's most outstanding characteristic. 'Don't let's talk about him any more,' she said at last. 'I'm simply employed by him. His character has nothing whatever to do with me.'

But as Hettie turned and stared at her directly, she busied herself with picking energetically at the seam and it was with a shake of her head that Hettie slipped her tray of sausage rolls into the oven.

On the following morning the children from Laureston School arrived for their lesson. As usual, Senga accompanied them and she and Blane strolled off together while Briony took over the children.

For the first time since her adventures with the bicycle Sandra appeared, and immediately Briony was struck by the improvement in her. The episode seemed to have made Sandra a person of importance among her young friends. And, to Briony's amazement, girls who previously had treated Sandra with contempt now spoke to her quite deferentially.

There was also the fact that, thanks to the private lessons Briony had given her, Sandra's riding had improved so much that she was able to take her place among the others with a measure of self-confidence. It was doubtful if she would ever develop a good style; she simply wasn't a born rider, but at least, she was no longer a misfit.

When the lesson was over Sandra eagerly approached Briony. 'I've written to Daddy and asked him to buy Teddy, so that he can be a companion to Snowy—that's my white pony at home, you know. I think he must be lonely when I'm away at school and Teddy would be company for him. I'm sure Mr Lennox will agree. He can always get another donkey, can't he?'

Briony could hardly restrain a laugh at Sandra's new air of self-confidence. Well, at least, she was thinking, Sandra was one person she wouldn't have to worry about any more!

Briony caught sight of Blane and Senga standing outside the loosebox in which Golden Sovereign was kept. Senga was feeding him lumps of sugar and when, a little later, Briony went into the next loosebox she could hear Senga say, 'Golden Sovereign seems very restless.'

'Yes,' Blane replied, 'he hasn't been getting the exercise he should have. I'll see he gets a good run each day after this. Although, come to think of it, I have to go into Aberdeen in the morning. That will be another half day lost.'

'But what's been happening?' Senga asked.

'Things fell behind a little while Briony was off. The boys—and myself for that matter—were loaded with work.'

'Oh yes, invaluable Briony!' Senga laughed lightly. 'I hope she doesn't get to know that the Lennox Riding School quite falls apart at the seams when she's not here.'

What would Blane have to say to this? Briony wondered, as she tied up a hay net in the adjoining stable. But he chose to ignore the remark. 'We'll just have to make it up to Golden Sovereign,' he told her.

'I was only joking,' Senga said quickly. 'I know how things were with you while she was away. But now that she's back what about our having that celebration dinner we were so much looking forward to? At least *I* was, and I hope you were too! Now that she's here again you'll be able to take an evening off. You owe it to me, you know. After all, I did win for you.'

And as Briony left the loosebox she could hear Blane saying, 'Let me see, what would be the best evening——'

CHAPTER TWELVE

On the following morning Briony packed a haversack with her purchases. Hettie's baking had proved to be a resounding success. But she had considered Briony's offerings just a bit too sparse for what she termed 'two growing boys', and had included a napkin packed with ham and tomato sandwiches. She had also added some bottles of her own special home-made ginger beer. She insisted too there was nothing boys liked better than trifles with genuine cream, and on the previous evening she had set about and made these up in small plastic cartons, and placed them in the fridge to set for the morning.

Briony smiled wryly as she hitched the haversack across her shoulder. If the boys really consumed as much as Hettie had provided they would be completely unable to do a stroke of work during the rest of the morning, she decided.

When she arrived at Birchfields she stored the haversack in a cupboard in the tack room that was seldom used and immediately set to work getting through her chores as quickly as possible.

Before it was time for the morning break, she had cleared her work load, and felt entitled to go to the tack room a little earlier than usual. She cleared the table of brushes, tins of saddle-soap and the odds and ends of tack, metal polish and vaseline which usually littered it. On the surface she laid sheets of brightly patterned wrapping paper, on which she arrayed the goodies she had brought. From the shelf on which they usually rested she took the chipped mugs they used at morning break.

As the two boys came in, she was rewarded by the look of astonished delight which came into Johnny's face as he spotted the pink and white iced birthday cake prominently displayed, flanked on each side by bottles of ginger beer and surrounded by the assorted goodies.

'Well, this is something I didn't expect,' he exclaimed, rubbing his hands in anticipation. 'Now that the boss has gone to Aberdeen, we can have a good tuck-in!'

'All the same, we'd better not delay over our break,' Andy said cautiously. 'You never know—he might come back early, and he's not in too good a humour these days, as we know.'

Johnny switched on the transistor. 'We may as well look on the bright side! He may be delayed.'

'After all, it won't take us so much longer to get through this than it would to take our ordinary break,' Briony interposed.

But here she proved to be wrong. Because, in spite of Andy's pessimism, they felt relaxed and in a festive mood.

'This is the first cheerful thing that's happened in ages,' Johnny remarked as they got around to the cake-cutting part of the feast. They were laughing and chatting as if they hadn't a care in the world when, as the picnic was over, Johnny pushed back the table and invited Briony to join him in a waltz to the blaring music from the transistor. He was so happy that, although Briony was increasingly aware that they had far exceeded their break time, she hadn't the heart to call a halt to the festivities.

They were, however, to receive a rude awakening.

As Johnny spun her around in a breathtaking climax to the dance, there was the sound of firm footsteps, and a shadow fell across the doorway. They came to a sudden halt as though frozen by Blane's unexpected appearance.

With a few swift strides he crossed to the transistor

and roughly switched it off. When he turned, his face
was dark with anger. 'And just what's going on here?'
he began. He glanced at his watch. 'Do you realise what
time it is?' And then his eyes narrowed as they fell upon
the remainder of the feast and the table pushed up
against the wall. 'And what's this?' he asked blankly.

'It was all my idea,' Briony said faintly, as the two
boys stood in embarrassed silence. 'It's Johnny's birthday and I got a few extra things to celebrate.'

'So you took advantage of the fact that I was going
into Aberdeen, to hold a party!' he gritted. 'In future,
don't hold celebrations on my time!'

Sheepishly the two boys edged towards the yard, and
Briony, to her dismay, found herself alone with a grim-
faced Blane. Nervously she began to crunch up the
empty plastic cartons and to thrust them into the oil-
drum that served as a waste-paper basket.

'You can do that afterwards,' he told her quickly. 'In
the meanwhile get on with your work!' And turning, he
strode from the tack room.

Left alone, surrounded by the debris of the party,
Briony's nervousness disappeared with a rush and was
replaced by furious anger. In defiance of his instructions
she began to gather together the plates and mugs, and
dump them on the shelves. Then, seizing the coloured
papers, she rolled them into a ball. How typical of him,
she thought furiously. After all, it wasn't as though they
were in the habit of wasting their time or lounging
around the tack room. In fact, the boys and herself had
more work than they could handle. Surely, for once,
Blane could have turned a blind eye!

As she crossed the yard, still seething with resentment,
she came upon Andy.

'I don't know what the boss is thinking of, giving the
Shetlands to Johnny,' Andy told her gloomily. 'After
all, he can't manage everything—and neither can I, for
that matter!'

'He took the Shetlands away from me out of spite,' Briony exclaimed furiously, 'and Johnny simply hates having them. I think the best thing I can do is take them on again, and——'

'You'd better not,' Andy interposed. 'The boss made a big point of Johnny having them. You'll get the sack for sure, if you don't toe the line.'

'Well, what way can I help, then?' Briony asked, exasperated.

'I only wish you could exercise the palomino,' he sighed. 'He's fidgety and restless. He hasn't got enough exercise for the past few days. But of course, there's no question of your doing that.'

Immediately Briony took up the challenge. 'Why shouldn't I exercise him?' she demanded. 'After all, I was told when I started work here that I'd have to do anything a stableboy can undertake.'

'But you won't be able to manage him!' Andy protested. 'He's not one of your Shetland ponies, you know,' he added with a grin.

'Senga MacNeil rides him,' Briony flashed.

Andy nodded, in his slow, stolid way. 'Yes, but she's much more experienced. And, to be straight with you,' he added bluntly, 'you're not as good a rider as Senga.'

In her heart Briony knew he was speaking the truth, but she would not admit it. She kept arguing with Andy with feminine persistence, and eventually he gave in.

'All right, then,' he said at last resignedly, 'but stay inside the grounds. Take the path behind the Dutch barn and you'll be able to give him a good gallop on the level, and get some of the steam out of him.'

She had no sooner mounted than she realised that Andy had been right, for she found that Golden Sovereign was jibbing and prancing with nervous tossings of his head. Her own nervousness had somehow conveyed itself to the animal, for although she tried to hold him with all her strength, she was barely able to control him.

As she came level with the Dutch barn, she caught a glimpse of Blane mounted on the Hanoverian. But she did not know if he had seen her because she had enough to do trying to control the palomino as it waltzed sideways as though in a complicated dance. A moment later and she had reached the flat area behind the barn and was able to let Golden Sovereign have his head. He surged forward so suddenly that she was almost unseated.

Immediately her nervousness changed to exhilaration. How wonderful to ride a powerful horse like this, she thought, as the ground seemed to fly away beneath his heels. She delighted in the speed of this wonderful animal as the turf flew behind his bounding hooves.

It was only when she began to try to rein him in that she discovered that he had no intention of obeying her. Golden Sovereign was aware that she did not have the authority of Senga. A horse of this calibre was away beyond her skill, and the palomino was only too well aware of it. Briony pulled frantically on the reins as she realised the animal was bolting with her, but her exertions proved useless.

Vaguely she remembered instructions she had once received about what to do in such a situation. Pulling frantically on the reins was exactly the wrong thing to do. Instead of gradually and smoothly slackening the reins before tightening them, she found that she relaxed them too suddenly and her mount took this as encouragement to put on even more speed.

She remembered too, with growing panic, that a horse is at least eight times as strong as its rider and that trying to pull in a bolting horse is useless.

Feeling helpless, she was overcome by panic and gave a shriek of pure terror. Golden Sovereign laid his ears back and seemed to fly along at even greater speed, while Briony concentrated on trying to keep her seat.

It was then she heard the sound of galloping hooves behind her, and caught a glimpse of the Hanoverian coming up behind. Gradually it gained on her. Side by side the two horses galloped at breakneck speed. After a while it dawned on Briony that Blane was forcing the palomino to run in circles which gradually decreased in size. There came a slackening of speed and Briony found to her relief that the danger was at last over.

But the Golden Sovereign had still one last trick up his sleeve. In the centre of the field was a marshy patch of turf. Here he decided finally to stop, but drew up so suddenly that Briony flew over his head and found herself with her face and hair forced into the sticky clinging mud.

In a second Blane had slid down from the saddle of the Hanoverian and was by her side. She tried to wipe away the tears that made little channels through the mud that coated her face.

'Are you hurt?' he exclaimed.

'No, there's nothing the matter with me,' she told him quaveringly, feeling completely demoralised.

'But you're crying,' he insisted.

'I'm crying because I'm angry!' she burst out.

For a moment he looked at her in silence, then, flinging back his head, went into roars of laughter.

Disconcerted by his reaction, Briony gazed at him speechlessly, aware of what a spectacle she must present, her face coated with mud, her hair in sticky dripping wisps.

'I'm not going to ask you why you did that,' he said, as he helped her to her feet, 'because I know it was my own fault. After all, you did want to hold on to the Shetlands. But it was a very foolish thing to do. The palomino could easily have broken your neck.'

He pulled a silk scarf from about his neck and gently mopped her face. 'Do you know,' he said quietly, 'that little nose of yours looks even cuter covered with mud.'

Unnerved by her experience and undecided what attitude she should take, she found herself smiling tremulously. 'I remember when I first came I boasted I could do everything the boys could do. And I wanted to prove it to you. Well, it seems I can't after all. It makes me feel a bit of an impostor.'

As they walked towards the stables with Blane leading their mounts, his arm was about her waist. It was true her legs still felt decidedly wobbly. All the same she hoped neither of the boys would be around when they reached the stableyard.

To her relief there was no sign of them.

'I think it might be as well if you got some of that mud off,' Blane told her. 'At present you're not much of an advert for the Lennox Riding School. Why don't you go up to the house and get Jean McPhee to open up the flat. After all, someone might as well have the use of it. Your godmother apparently didn't find it up to her standards.'

Briony regarded him uncertainly. Now that his comforting arm was no longer around her waist, all her old doubts and suspicions rushed back. She remembered Hettie's bitterness when she had spoken of how Blane had schemed to get her out of the flat. If only she could dismiss her nagging doubts about him, she thought miserably, as she slowly walked towards the house.

When Briony presented herself at the kitchen door, Mrs McPhee received her without the smallest surprise. 'Looks like you've had a nasty fall,' she remarked equably, when Briony asked if she could tidy up and explained that Blane had directed her to use the flat.

The housekeeper unhooked a key from a board and led the way around the house and up the stairs. She shook her head regretfully as she opened the door. 'Seems a shame that such a lovely place should be left unoccupied!' she remarked as she led the way towards the bathroom. 'Mr Blane spent a mint of money on this—and now look at it. Not, mind you,' she added, 'that I ever neglect the place. In case Mrs Gillies should ever turn up and want it again, I keep it spick and span,' she said gravely.

And, looking about her, Briony had to agree. Everything shone and sparkled with freshness; the snow-white tiled walls, the turquoise bathroom suite with its gleaming porcelain fittings.

The housekeeper switched on an electric heater and after a few moments turned on the taps in the wash-basin and steaming water immediately gushed out. 'It beats me why she left as she did. Everything had been thought of, as you can see.' She sighed. 'Not, mind you, that it was altogether her fault, for I was a bit snappy at times. But then she was provoking, if you don't mind me saying so.'

She reached in a cupboard and produced soft towels and a tablet of delicately scented soap.

Now was the time to get to the bottom of the mystery concerning Hettie's exodus from the flat, Briony thought, and she decided to take the bull by the horns and face the housekeeper with Hettie's complaints.

'My godmother says Mr Lennox wanted her out of the flat, but instead of asking her to leave in a straight-forward way, he put you up to showing her she was unwelcome.'

Mrs McPhee straightened and looked at her in aston-ishment. 'But that's not true,' she said flatly. 'Mr Blane was very forbearing, in my opinion. You see——' She hesitated, and then said in a rush. 'Mrs Gillies is a very interfering sort of body, and she was always down in the main part of the house and in the kitchen telling me how she thought things ought to be done and generally meddling with the running of the house. At first I took no notice, but when she saw that I wasn't carrying out her instructions, she complained to Mr Blane. Well, I tried to soothe her down, but it was no use, she still kept poking her nose into concerns that weren't hers, and in the end I told her off,' she added, looking a little guilty. 'I know I shouldn't have been so straightforward, but it really got on my nerves after a while, especially as I pride myself on being a good housekeeper and Mr Blane had never any complaints against me.'

Briony nodded. The picture was only too clear. It was easy to imagine Hettie, bored and with nothing to distract her, invading the lower part of the house and generally causing chaos with her interfering and dominating personality. 'I think I understand,' she said quietly, 'but, of course, my godmother was resentful about having to leave Birchfields. I don't think, no matter what Mr Lennox did for her, that she would have been satisfied.'

The housekeeper nodded sympathetically. 'Yes, poor body! I used to feel for her because she must have been lonely up here on her own. Perhaps she's better off where she is, down in the village with people around.'

After she had gone, Briony washed her hair and patted it dry in the thick soft towels, until it fell in loose gleaming waves almost to her shoulders. After her conversation with Jean McPhee she felt a wonderful feeling of relief. Blane had not put the housekeeper up to getting rid of Hettie—that was all that mattered.

As she went into the house she was surprised to see Blane, hands in pockets, striding up and down the hall. A thick rug near the door had prevented him hearing her approach and for a moment she paused, her hand on the door watching him, aware that her heart was beating fast at the sight of his broad sturdy figure. Would she always feel this surge of happiness when she caught sight of him? she wondered. And, if so, what future misery she was saving up for herself!

He swung around as he sensed her presence. 'Ah, there you are. I've been waiting for you.'

She moved forward and as they faced each other an awkward silence fell. His eyes scanned her hair and his brown hand touched it lightly. 'Why don't you always wear your hair that way? You look like an enchanted princess.'

She mustn't let her feelings betray her, Briony told herself. It was important to remember that it was Senga he would marry. 'It's time I got back to work,' she said with an attempt at lightness. 'I've spent enough time titivating myself.'

Immediately his manner changed. 'So I'm being put in my place, is that it? No idle compliments for Miss Briony Walton!'

'Oh no, I don't mean that!' she said quickly—too quickly and eagerly, she thought regretfully. 'It's just that—well——'

She dared not tell him that she dreaded finding herself once more—as she had with Jeremy Warne—at the losing end of a romance. The words that came so easily and casually were inclined to embed themselves in her heart. How was Blane to know how eagerly she longed for his approval? She mustn't fall for his passing mood.

But as she spoke she had turned and scanned his face earnestly!

He put his hands on her shoulders and drew her towards him. 'Why are you so mistrustful, Briony?' he asked, his voice gentle.

She looked at him warily. Was she so obvious then? Had Jeremy's betrayal left a lasting scar? 'I don't know what you mean,' she said uncertainly, avoiding his eyes.

He shook his head. 'You forget I'm Scottish. Haven't you heard that we Scots have the gift of second sight? There's something about you that tells me you were hurt badly at some time.'

She tried to laugh his remark away. 'Now that is something I can't believe! You, with second sight—you, of all people! You're much too down-to-earth and practical.'

'That's just where you're wrong! If you were ever to go away from Birchfields I think I'd see you in every nook and cranny of the place.'

Again her eyes scanned his face.

His voice had had a cadence she hadn't heard in it before. He was teasing her, she guessed, but it was a loving teasing that she found irresistible. Slowly he drew her towards him and this time she didn't resist. He was in love with her, she realised, with sudden overwhelming joy. There could be no mistaking it now that his lips were on hers. Everything seemed to fade into the background. She was only aware that what she had imagined was her love for Jeremy was a pale shadow of what she now felt for this man. When at last he released her, she gave a little sigh of blissful ecstasy.

His arm was about her waist, her head was against his shoulder, when Senga walked through the open door.

As a shaft of light illuminated them for a moment she stared unbelievingly. Then her face stiffened with a mixture of rage and bewilderment. 'I seem to be interrupting something,' she said, her voice grating. 'But don't let it trouble you, Briony! I've no objection to Blane flirting with the hired help if he feels like it.'

Briony could feel her face flush crimson at the insult. But Blane regarded Senga steadily and as her glance flashed from one face to the other, she seemed to grasp from their expressions that this was no passing thing.

She gave a short bitter laigh. 'Just as well I'm leaving Laureston! It's very obvious now I'd be very much de trop if I stayed on.'

Briony, feeling awkward and for some reason or other slightly guilty, drew away from Blane and pushed her hair back.

'Oh, don't mind me,' Senga said with a tight smile. 'It's quite obvious that you two have got it badly. Just as well, I suppose, that I've had a flaming row with

Anderson, and we both decided the time had come to part. Still, I thought I could depend on you, Blane!'

'And so you can,' he returned quietly. 'If there's anything I can do to help you, let me know.'

'How awfully sweet of you,' Senga sneered. 'I had thought of living near Laureston, but I think I'd better make a clean break and leave Abergour. I believe in cutting my losses, you know.' And with that she turned and walked swiftly through the door.

When Briony returned to the cottage that evening Hettie had a cosy fire crackling in the sitting-room and, as usual, a delicious meal ready for her.

Afterwards, as she was sipping coffee by the fireside, she became aware that although Hettie, seated in her rocking chair on the other side of the fire, appeared absorbed in her sewing, now and then she would steal a covert glance in her direction.

Immediately she was defensive. She must not betray her happiness, because she was only too well aware of what Hettie's reaction would be should she guess the truth.

'You seem very pleased with yourself,' Hettie said at last, unable to control her curiosity. 'Your lord and master must have been in a particularly good mood today.'

Briony busied herself with pouring another cup of coffee before answering. Then she said with a great air of indifference, 'Oh yes, I'm out of his black books at last and I'm to get the Shetlands back again.'

'Now that's very obliging of him, isn't it!' said Hettie dryly as she poked the fire belligerently.

'Have you heard that Senga MacNeil is going to leave Laureston?' Briony asked, hoping to divert Hettie's attention from Blane.

Hettie laid down the poker and looked up in amazement. 'Why on earth is she doing that? I heard it was all fixed she was to marry Blane Lennox. Everyone in the village was sure of it.'

'It seems she had a row with Miss Anderson,' Briony said carefully. 'I don't think they got on very well. The headmistress is so very prim and proper and Senga's so independent.'

Hettie sniffed. 'If she'd any sense she'd control that temper of hers. Miss Anderson may have her faults, but she's not a bad sort, and Senga may travel far before she does any better.'

To Briony's relief, she could see that Hettie's mind had drifted off on the subject of Senga's future.

After a thoughtful silence, Hettie said suddenly, 'Oh, by the way, I forgot to tell you that there's a letter for you. It came by the morning post.' She reached down an envelope from behind the clock on the mantelshelf.

Briony, her mind still on the events of the day, received it without particular interest. She glanced at it unseeingly for a moment until, with a sense of shock, she recognised Jeremy's unmistakable handwriting. What on earth could Jeremy have to say to her? she wondered in alarm.

In spite of Hettie's curiosity, there and then she tore open the envelope. Her eyes scanned the lines. He was going to drop in on her at Abergour, he told her. There was something very important he had to speak to her about.

'Although I expect you've guessed,' he continued, 'that I want to propose again. The old Jeremy is quite dead—you'll find me a different person. I simply must see you. Please don't refuse. I can't tell you how miserable I've been. I realise what a dreadful mistake I've made, but I simply can't believe that it's too late.'

CHAPTER THIRTEEN

BRIONY read the lines with growing dismay.

But it *was* too late, she was thinking. Jeremy simply couldn't come to Abergour. His presence would be known in every corner of the village within a few minutes of his arrival.

'What's wrong?' Hettie asked. 'Not bad news, I hope.'

'It's Jeremy Warne—he wants to call. He seems to think we can start off again where we left off.' Briony glanced at her watch. 'I'll have to try to phone him before he leaves the office, and let him know it's absolutely no go.'

'But why not?' Hettie put in quickly. 'It's nothing out of the usual for young people to have a tiff and then make up again—especially when they're engaged. You're too stiffnecked, Briony. You'll never get a husband if you keep up this attitude, I can tell you.'

'Then I'll do without one!' Briony retorted heatedly. 'Anyway, it isn't a tiff, as you call it. He flung me over, which is an entirely different matter. As far as I'm concerned it's all completely finished. I want nothing more to do with him.'

'That's what you say now,' Hettie retorted, 'but sooner or later you'll regret being so stubborn. After all, he has a good job at present and is going places, so it seems. You'll not find anyone like him around these parts, I can tell you.'

In spite of herself, Briony found her lips curving in a smile. But Blane was in love with her, and the knowledge was balm to her heart. To her now Jeremy was simply a rather tiresome complication. She would phone him immediately and tell him in no uncertain terms that there could be no possibility of her meeting him again.

'I'll have to rush, Hettie,' she said a little impatiently, 'or I'll miss Jeremy at the office.'

Hettie shrugged resignedly. 'I can see your mind's made up. I just hope you won't regret it later, that's all I say.'

'Don't worry, I shan't,' Briony called back confidently, as, slipping on her coat, she sped down the path. Sooner or later Hettie would have to know she loved Blane Lennox, but in the meanwhile Briony resolutely put the problem behind her and concentrated on what she would say to Jeremy.

To her relief the phone booth outside the little post office was unoccupied and she had very little trouble getting connected with Jeremy's office. But the girl at the switchboard seemed doubtful if she could get in touch with him. There was a delay, then came the girl's voice, 'I'm afraid Mr Warne has already gone.'

Briony felt her heart sink. She could leave a message, of course, telling him not to call, but, knowing how tenacious he could be when it came to getting his own way, she doubted if it would have the smallest effect on him. There was only one thing for it, she decided, and that was to call on him in Aberdeen on the following morning.

It was still dark when Briony got up on the following morning. Her trip to Aberdeen wouldn't take much time, she thought. She'd simply tell Jeremy exactly where he stood and return immediately to Abergour.

She intended catching the first bus from the village and dressed as quickly as she could. But Hettie was exasperatingly slow in preparing breakfast: her mind on Briony's forthcoming interview with Jeremy, she insisted that to fortify herself for the coming confrontation Briony should have a good Scottish breakfast, as she called it.

When this was over Briony had no time to go up to Birchfields and explain that although she would not be able to come in that morning, she would be back in good time for the treasure hunt. Instead, she decided to phone from the kiosk outside the post-office and leave a message with Mrs McPhee.

But when she got through it was Blane's deep voice that answered. She plunged into her explanation before her courage could desert her. 'This is Briony, and I'm calling to let you know I shan't be able to come in this morning. But I definitely won't fail this afternoon.'

There was a silence at the other end of the line, then he said, 'Then it must be something pretty important, considering we're holding the treasure hunt today.'

'I know, and I wouldn't have had it happen for the world, but you see, something completely unexpected has come up.'

'If it's completely unexpected, then you can tell yourself you have a prior engagement,' came Blane's voice. He spoke equably, but it was clear he was insisting she should put in an appearance. 'There's a lot to be done this morning and it's important you should be here early,' he went on. 'After all, we've all put work into this—you especially.'

'I'm sorry,' she replied desperately. 'I have to go into Aberdeen, but I'll be back as soon as I possibly can.'

Again there was silence, but she could sense his burning anger.

'I see you're determined to have your own way. Very well, I've nothing more to say!' And he put down the receiver with a click of finality—as though, she thought uneasily, he was dismissing her completely from his plans.

When she came out of the phone booth, the bus was already drawn up and she had to rush to the bus stop. There was quite a queue, mostly women, all eagerly chatting in anticipation of their day's shopping in

Aberdeen, and clutching large baskets and shopping bags. Quickly the front seats in the bus were filled and Briony found herself relegated to the very back row.

As they passed the gates of Birchfields she saw that the lights were on outside the stables and for an instant she caught a glimpse of Andy and Johnny moving about. Then, as she glanced through the back window, she saw Blane's big grey car coming along the drive. She knew he was coaching a rider who had entered for a competition to be held very shortly. He lived in a large estate beyond the village, so she was a little surprised to see that, instead of turning off, the big grey car appeared to be following the bus. Then it gained speed and swept past. It was unlikely that Blane would be going into Aberdeen today of all days, she thought vaguely, leaving Andy and Johnny to deal with the details in connection with the treasure hunt. Then she dismissed the incident from her mind, concentrating on the unpleasant interview that lay ahead.

As the bus approached Aberdeen she was struck again by the way the town had grown: buildings which at one time had been quite outside the city were now swallowed up in the growth of this boom town.

She arrived in Aberdeen too early for her interview with Jeremy, so she went into the terminus restaurant and ordered a cup of coffee, lingering over it as long as possible in an effort to kill time. Surrounding her, she could hear accents from all parts of the world—especially American: there was the slow soft speech of the Texan and the more rapid, crisper speech of the north. Aberdeen had become a great international centre that drew in all who came near it. No wonder Jeremy was so elated to be part of this busy and exciting city that could hold such opportunities for someone as ambitious as himself. It was so completely different from Abergour that for a moment it was hard to believe that only a few miles separated them.

She went along in good time to his office to catch
him as he came in and took her seat in one of the comfortable chairs facing the switchboard. She glanced
around, remembering with disbelief the misery of that
last meeting. How strange that this time she would be
able to meet him without the smallest heartbreak! No
doubt it would be a very unpleasant encounter, yet her
heart would not be involved. He had no place now in
her life.

She caught sight of him immediately he came in and
saw him exercising his usual charm on the girls at the
switchboard, waving to them as he approached with that
half-smile that used to make her heart beat faster. Now
she regarded him with the eyes of a stranger and realised
that he used his charm as a weapon, a means of pro-
moting his overwhelming ambition.

'Briony!' His voice held a flattering warmth, and once
again that brilliant smile seemed to encompass her.

'You got my letter?' he said eagerly.

'Yes, that's why I'm here,' she told him quietly.

He glanced at his watch. 'Let's go out for a cup of
coffee. I'm pretty well my own boss now, you know. No
one holds a stopwatch over Jeremy Warne, I can assure
you of that!'

'I can stay only a few minutes,' she told him. 'It's just
to tell you that you mustn't call at Abergour. There's
no point in it any more.'

He took a seat beside her, his hand covering hers. 'I
don't know what you mean,' he said, puzzled.

'Simply that I don't want you to come to Abergour.
You'd be going to all that trouble for nothing. You
must know there's nothing between us now.'

She saw the look of astonishment creep into his eyes.
'But Briony, you don't understand! If you only knew
what a different person I am! I've thought so hard about
you. I made a terrible mistake, and I'm ready to admit
it. Give me a chance to prove you're the only one in the

world for me—and always have been. Oh, I know I was a bit carried away by that Texan girl, but that's all in the past. I've not met anyone since who can hold a candle to you. I'll make it all up to you, just you see!'

She could hear the confidence return to his voice. 'Jeremy,' she said quietly, 'you simply don't understand. Things are different for me now. I've fallen in love.'

'Fallen in love!' he repeated incredulously. 'Don't tell me you've fallen for a crofter in Abergour!'

'No, not a crofter,' she told him, trying to keep her temper in check. 'But if he was, and I loved him, I'd marry him.'

For the first time, she realised that he had not for one moment suspected that there would be another man in her life.

'He happens to keep a riding school,' she told him evenly, 'and it's doing very well too,' she added, a note of pride creeping into her voice.

'No doubt, by Abergour standards, he's a wealthy man,' Jeremy said acidly.

'He's not wealthy. But then that doesn't make much difference to me.'

'Obviously! But then you were always a romantic little fool, weren't you, Briony?' Then, with a rush, he added, 'You're not really going to marry this man, are you?'

'Yes, if he asks me.'

'I see, so he hasn't popped the question yet! Suppose he doesn't, is there any chance you and I could get together again? I've made contacts here and now I have the chance to go to Houston, Texas. There are strong connections between the two cities. There are plenty of Scots living there. You wouldn't be lonely. You could have every luxury you set your heart on, and a really good time. What's more, don't tell me you wouldn't be thrilled to be married to a man who was on the way up. That's important to any wife. And I'm not just building castles in the air—I've got a solid job lined up.'

'You don't understand,' she told him, almost wearily. 'That's not the sort of life I want. Don't you realise, I'm in love and, as far as I'm concerned, that comes before everything.'

Jeremy's eyes narrowed. 'Very well!' He got to his feet. 'As I said, you were always a romantic little fool. You deserve what you get. It would serve you right if this hero of yours left you in the lurch. Mark my words, my girl, you'll live to regret turning me down!'

Briony looked after him as he walked towards the lifts, like a petulant schoolboy. How immature he seemed, compared to Blane! She hadn't noticed that before. But then she hadn't really been in love; infatuated, perhaps, and dazzled by her first love, as most girls were.

For a moment she sat still, feeling emotionally drained. The meeting she had so dreaded was a thing of the past. She must look to the future now and, first of all, she must get back to Abergour as soon as possible. She would take a taxi, she decided. It was the quickest way of getting there and she owed it to Blane to give him as much assistance as possible.

She began to walk along Union Street, her eyes searching out a taxi, and as she did so a car drew level with her, keeping pace with her for a few steps. Startled, she turned her head, and found herself looking into Blane's eyes.

He pushed open the door. 'Get in,' he said laconically.

Startled by his unexpected appearance, she obeyed automatically.

'You seem surprised to see me in Aberdeen today,' he said dryly as he set off once more.

'I—I didn't expect to see you,' she stammered. 'I thought you'd be busy. I mean—with the treasure hunt, and—and——' She stopped in confusion. She glanced at his profile and saw that it was tight with anger.

He didn't speak again until they had pulled free of the city. Then, as though he could no longer contain his rage, he gritted, 'So this was the important engagement! This was what you had to let me down for—Jeremy Warne!'

'You must have followed me,' she gasped. 'I saw the car come along the drive this morning as the bus was leaving Abergour, but I didn't dream you'd——'

'You didn't dream I'd follow you, is that it? You don't seem to understand that when you love someone you learn to interpret every expression on their face and every tone of their voice, and this morning there was something about your story that rang a warning bell for me!'

'But—but it wasn't fair! You had no right to follow me!' she said in a feeble attempt to assert herself.

'Oh yes, I had!' he said harshly. 'I thought you were in love with me, I had to know exactly how I stood.'

'If you love a person, you trust them!' she cried. 'You should have trusted——'

But he broke in, 'When you love someone you're afraid that somewhere there's someone who's going to try to steal what's closest to your heart. Perhaps, even in spite of yourself, this Jeremy Warne has influenced you. I've seen him, I know the type.'

'You know that's not true,' she said hotly.

'Isn't it? It seems he's a wealthy man—or at least on the way to being one. My future lies in Abergour. With him, you'll have the world before you. What girl could resist? Do you think I haven't thought of the difference between us? Besides, he's nearer to your own age. I don't forget either that this Jeremy Warne is young and good-looking. Compared to him, I have nothing much to offer you, have I?'

'How dare you!' Briony blazed. 'I'd rather walk than listen to another word. Stop the car!' she demanded.

'I'll do nothing of the sort,' he told her.

She glanced at him. The bitter rage which had engulfed him had disappeared as quickly as it had come, and he was his usual self. He had told her he could follow every nuance of her voice, but she herself, she realised, would never understand this enigmatic man; his sudden black moods, and equally sudden tenderness.

She turned her head away and gazed blankly through the window. In his jealous rage Blane did not trust her love. Very well, she would not try to convince him of it! She would offer no explanation.

But as they drove back in silence to Abergour she felt her defences crumble and she slid down in the seat as misery engulfed her. Bleakly she surveyed the future. Was she once again to be on the losing side when she allowed herself to fall in love?

As Blane drew up outside Amulree Briony didn't wait until the car came to a halt. Pushing open the door, she jumped out and hurried up the path. Hettie, who was weeding in the garden, looked up with open-mouthed amazement as Briony sped like a hurricane into the cottage.

Her first instinct was to indulge in a good cry, but firmly she held back the tears. She had no intention of turning up at the Riding School with red-rimmed eyes and tear-stained cheeks. Rather she determined to show Blane that his behaviour during the morning hadn't got her down.

She would look her best, she decided, as she opened her wardrobe. No tatty slacks and scuffed boots—she would wear a tweed hacking jacket and jodhpurs. She selected a polo-necked sweater from the tallboy and polished her boots until they shone like glass. She combed her hair back and took her velvet riding cap from the wardrobe shelf.

When she was dressed she looked at her reflection in the mirror with satisfaction. She looked smart and dashing, she decided, and not at all the subdued culprit Blane probably expected to turn up.

When she went downstairs again, Hettie was sitting at the table slicing Dundee cake and with a large brown teapot under the cosy. She looked up, her eyes opening in astonishment. 'My goodness, you do look smart! I've never seen you dressed up in that kit before. I must say it suits you down to the ground.'

'It's not the sort of thing one would wear when mucking out stables at the Lennox Riding School,' Briony agreed dryly. 'By the way, you were quite right about Blane Lennox! He's the most arrogant man I've ever come across. I expect this is going to be my last day there, so I may as well put on as good a show as possible.'

'Does this mean you're throwing up your job?' Hettie asked, laying down her knife in surprise.

'Well, you should be pleased at any rate. You never particularly liked him,' Briony reminded her.

'Oh, I don't know, perhaps I was a bit hasty.' Hettie looked a bit shamefaced. 'He's not as bad as I thought, and he has been a good boss as far as you're concerned. He has a bossy manner, I admit, and can be very arrogant at times. All the same, that doesn't mean to say he wouldn't make a good husband for a girl, and although I said nothing about it, I got the feeling right from the start that he was falling for you. And don't tell me you're not keen on him, because I know you are!'

'Well, I'm not keen on him any more,' Briony retorted. 'We had the most awful quarrel and he let me know all too clearly that he doesn't trust me.'

Hettie sighed. 'Why don't you sit down and have a cup of tea and a piece of cake? You'll feel better afterwards.'

'I wish you'd stop talking to me as if I were a child, Hettie!' Briony said petulantly, although, now that she came to think of it, she did feel that a cup of Hettie's hot strong tea and a piece of rich Dundee cake would be very welcome.

'We all know Blane Lennox is hard to get on with,' Hettie said thoughtfully, 'but you won't get a better job around these parts, as you know very well.'

'It doesn't look as if I'm going to have much choice anyway,' Briony told her in a subdued voice. 'I'm pretty certain I'm going to get the sack.'

Hettie looked at her sympathetically. 'Well, never mind! You can stay on here as long as you like. You know you're welcome, don't you?'

Mutely Briony nodded. 'I know, Hettie. And you're simply wonderful. But I couldn't impose on you. I'll probably be able to get a job in Aberdeen—sitting at a desk, I suppose,' she added disconsolately.

'Don't bother about it now,' Hettie told her. 'Finish your tea, and we'll talk about it some other time.'

When Briony arrived at the Riding School she was half disappointed, half relieved to find there was no sign of her imperious employer, and soon she was immersed in organising the children for the treasure hunt. They were wildly excited, and although she had anticipated some of the problems that might arise, when it came to the bit, everything was even worse than she had feared. Fierce squabbles burst out about the allocation of ponies, each child clinging adamantly to her own particular choice, and it took Briony all her diplomacy and patience to sort things out.

Eventually they set off, riding in pairs with the partners they had chosen. She accompanied them through a little copse of rowan trees, cautioning them to avoid low branches, but the children were so excited and talkative that she had difficulty in getting her message across. But gradually they became engrossed in deciphering the clues and settled down in earnest to try to find the treasure.

To Briony's delight it was Sandra and her partner

who discovered it in the oak tree, and with the two girls crowing with triumph over their find, she accompanied the children to the house for consolation prizes and the slap-up spread Jean McPhee had prepared.

They took their places at a long table laden with an assortment of trifles and jellies, crackers, cakes and big jugs of the raspberry-pink concoction so popular with children of their age. This was followed by home-made ice-cream. Soon they were tucking in heartily, discussing the day's events in high-pitched excitement.

As she looked at them Briony felt herself overcome with a cloud of depression. This would probably be her last day with the children. She would miss them dreadfully, she realised. Somehow it didn't seem possible that she wouldn't be turning up again at the Lennox Riding School in the darkness of an autumn morning with the lights of the stables outlining Andy and Johnny as they strode whistling about the yard. It had all become so familiar now. To her this place was a second home, and she couldn't even bring herself to imagine where she would be next. Some office, no doubt, tied to a desk all day!

She felt Jean McPhee glance at her with curiosity and realised that she was looking as dismal as she felt. She tried to smile. 'Well, the children seem to be having a good time, anyway,' she remarked. 'Would you like me to help you give out the consolation prizes before they go home?'

'Oh, I think I'll manage,' Jean McPhee answered, and then added hurriedly, 'Oh, I forgot, Mr Blane said he wants to see you in the office as soon as it's convenient.'

Briony nodded gloomily. Yes, just as she had thought! When the party was over she would get the sack, and that would be that! Better to go now, she thought, and get it over. No use putting off the evil moment. The sooner she started making her future plans the better.

The children, engrossed in their own interests, paid no attention as she slipped away.

Slowly she approached the office door, and when Blane told her to come in she squared her shoulders and tried to assume a look as blank and unemotional as possible.

When she went in she noticed with a little pang that he was standing as she always remembered him, hands clasped behind his back, gazing through one of the windows.

He swung around as she entered and for a moment they regarded each other wordlessly. When he spoke his voice sounded stiff and formal. 'I just want to say how pleased I am that you made such a success of the treasure hunt. I was keeping an eye on things and I noticed how wonderfully you managed the children.'

Startled and disconcerted by his words—they were completely unexpected—Briony stood confused and speechless.

Misunderstanding her reaction, he slowly turned once more towards the window. His voice was low when he spoke. 'It's natural you should feel resentful. I behaved appallingly badly. After all, you have the right to choose the life you want. Why shouldn't you visualise the future as something better than the Lennox Riding School? The world is before you. With Jeremy Warne you'll have all the luxuries a girl could want. Just let's say I was wildly jealous and lost my head. I don't expect you can forgive me, but at least I want you to know that no matter what you do or where you go, you'll always be the only one I really love. I expect you and I are a bit alike in certain ways. I thought I was in love too once, but it was only a faint reflection of the real thing. It was a sort of mirage,' he continued quietly, 'with no real substance or future.'

As his words penetrated her confused mind she felt

an uprush of happiness that seemed to overwhelm her like a great wave.

Before she knew what she had done she was by his side and his arms were around her. 'Since I met you, Jeremy has meant nothing to me,' she told him. 'But he wanted us to start all over again, as if nothing had happened. That's why I went to Aberdeen—to tell him nothing could possibly be the same again. Did you not guess that I was in love with you? I used to think the whole world must know how I felt about you.'

For a long moment they stood close in each other's arms. How wonderful to be loved as she was! A new beginning! A sort of springtime of the heart, she thought blissfully.

Harlequin Plus

A GREAT ROMANTIC POET

Briony's favorite poet is Lord Byron, one of the great Romantic poets of the nineteenth century. It is not difficult to fall under the spell of Byron's eloquently beautiful verse, as his stirring " She Walks in Beauty," reprinted below, will show.

She walks in beauty, like the night
 Of cloudless climes and starry skies;
And all that's best of dark and bright
 Meet in her aspect and her eyes;
Thus mellow'd to that tender light
 Which heaven to gaudy day denies.

One shade the more, one ray the less
 Had half impair'd the nameless grace
Which waves in every raven tress,
 Or softly lightens o'er her face;
Where thoughts serenely sweet express
 How pure, how dear their dwelling-place.

And on that cheek, and o'er that brow,
 So soft, so calm, yet eloquent,
The smiles that win, the tints that glow,
 That tell of days in goodness spent,
A mind at peace with all below,
 A heart whose love is innocent!

HELP HARLEQUIN PICK 1982's GREATEST ROMANCE!

We're taking a poll to find the most romantic couple (real, not fictional) of 1982. Vote for any one you like, but please vote and mail in your ballot today. As Harlequin readers, you're the real romance experts!

Here's a list of suggestions to get you started. Circle your choice, <u>or</u> print the names of the couple you think is the most romantic in the space below.

Prince of Wales / Princess of Wales

Luke / Laura (General Hospital stars)

Gilda Radner / Gene Wilder

Jacqueline Bisset / Alexander Godunov

Mark Harmon / Christina Raines

Carly Simon / Al Corley

Susan Seaforth / Bill Hayes

Burt Bacharach / Carole Bayer Sager

_____

(please print)

_____

_____

Please mail to: Maureen Campbell
               Harlequin Books
               225 Duncan Mill Road
               Don Mills, Ontario, Canada
               M3B 3K9

POLL-1